Breakdown

Cathy Sweeney

WEIDENFELD & NICOLSON

First published in Great Britain in 2024 by Weidenfeld & Nicolson,
an imprint of The Orion Publishing Group Ltd
Carmelite House, 50 Victoria Embankment
London EC4Y 0DZ

An Hachette UK Company

1 3 5 7 9 10 8 6 4 2

Epigraph on p.v: *Robinson* by Muriel Spark, 1958, published by Canongate
Books Ltd; reproduced by permission of David Higham Associates.

A CIP catalogue record for this book is
available from the British Library.

ISBN (Hardback) 978 1 4746 1851 9
ISBN (Export Trade Paperback) 978 1 4746 1852 6
ISBN (eBook) 978 1 4746 1854 0
ISBN (Audio) 978 1 4746 1860 1

Typeset by Input Data Services Ltd, Bridgwater, Somerset

Printed in Great Britain by Clays Ltd, Elcograf S.p.A.

MIX
Paper from
responsible sources
FSC® C104740

www.weidenfeldandnicolson.co.uk
www.orionbooks.co.uk

To JL

'Things mount up inside one, and then one has to perpetrate an outrage.'

Robinson, Muriel Spark, 1958

House

Mothers are not supposed to go on road trips.

Mothers can go on holidays, city breaks, outings, but not on road trips. It is women *without* children who go on road trips. When a Mother leaves home, she is expected to return, sooner or later, with shopping bags. And there are good reasons for this. Driving on a motorway, or travelling by train or bus or ferry, or taking a lift from a stranger, or spending a night in a cheap hotel, a Mother might take a break from the story that she is telling herself about the life that she is living.

And then what?

The morning I leave my comfortable home in the suburbs of Dublin and set out on a road trip is an ordinary Tuesday in November, sometime in that brief lull between Halloween being over and the drumroll to Christmas beginning. When the alarm goes, I hit the snooze button and lie there, wide awake in the darkness. I feel the same as I do every other morning: a bit stressed, a bit headachy, my gums sore from grinding my mouth guard in my dreams. Beside me, like a slow metronome, the breathing of a man deeply satisfied with his life; with his great wife and kids, his comfortable home and successful career, and the app on his Apple Watch telling him every night that he has reached his daily goals.

The day ahead is carved in marble. Get up. Get ready for work at a state secondary school. Make sure son is up. Drink coffee. Let the cat out. Drop son to school. Drive to work. Teach classes. Make small talk with colleagues. Pick up a bottle of wine on the way home. Make dinner. Pour wine.

Tidy up. Put a wash on. Avoid row with daughter. Remind husband to contact his mother about her test results. Have bath. Mess around on phone. Finish bottle of wine. Turn on TV in bedroom. Fall asleep.

But something snaps on that ordinary Tuesday in November. I don't feel like going to work. I don't feel like dropping my son to school. I don't even feel like letting the cat out.

Snooze time is up. I dress for work since work is where I *should* be going: black trousers, ankle boots, large white shirt, pale blue cashmere jumper, houndstooth coat with costume brooch. The trousers are tight after being dry-cleaned and I have to suck in to get the zip up. In the bathroom I brush my teeth, put on some make-up and run a brush through my hair. Downstairs, when I open the fridge for a bottle of water, there is a stench of garlic. The chorizo has been left out of its storage box again. In the living room a lamp is on and a tie is draped over the couch. On the coffee table, the remains of a cheese platter.

I grab my handbag and keys, let the front door shut behind me.

I have no idea that I will never come back.

In my memory there was a strange, unreal mood that morning I left. A stillness. Everything not just cold, but frozen, as though a bell jar had been placed over it. The footpaths. The road. The housing estate. Nothing moved, not even the leaves on the trees. Distant birdsong sounded like piped music and yellow windows hinted at activity yet to come, but not yet.

But quite likely the morning was not like that at all. Memory is the great filmmaker, gathering up fragments of mood and making them into images. When I think back to that morning now, I see it as a clip from a film in which I am the main character. I see myself in a silent landscape as though on old cine footage being projected onto a screen. I have watched the clip a million times. A blonde woman is standing on a doorstep, handbag on her shoulder, keys in her hand. It is dark outside but she is visible in street light. She walks down the driveway towards her black SUV, activating the alarm, but something interrupts, a voice calling from the road. She takes a few steps further down the driveway, folding her arms against the cold. The woman might be described as 'well-preserved' or good-looking 'for her age'. Maybe you think you know her. Or know her *type*.

I have played this clip so often, sometimes in colour, sometimes in black and white, trying to get a close-up shot, but I can never see the woman's face.

The door shuts and I am outside.

It is cold. Under the street lights, the trees appear bronze, and drops of rain hang from their leaves. I can hear birds chirring.

Around me, the estate is static. Each detached redbrick house exactly the same, though with 'distinctive' variations. Privet hedge or wall. Wrought iron gate or stone pillars. Wooden or metal number plates. A hanging basket or a potted bay leaf plant on either side of the porch. One of the houses has an early Christmas tree in its window, while a pumpkin sits on the step of another, its smile sunken and black.

A BMW halts just beyond our driveway. The window slides down and a hand emerges, waving enthusiastically back and forth.

—Hey, you! Long time no see.

The hand and the voice belong to my neighbour, Susan, on her way to the gym, her work suit dangling from a hanger in the back. My husband and I are friendly with her and her husband. Our children are the wrong ages to be friends, but they know each other.

I take a few steps down the driveway and say hello, folding my arms against the cold.

Susan's hair sits on the collar of her track top, shiny and tame. She is a big-shot lawyer. Her husband does something in theatre but seems to spend most of his time looking after their four children. Susan refers to him, usually while touching his arm, as 'the creative one'. She told me once when we were all a bit drunk that if there was a fire in her house, the first thing she would save would be her Dyson hairdryer.

—Everything OK?
—Fine, I say, but as I'm saying it I realise it's not true. Actually, no. Nothing is OK.
—What?

She starts to laugh. But when I say nothing more her mouth freeze frames, and she drives off.

A white gauze coats my SUV. I press the electronic key, sit in, put my handbag on the passenger seat. My whole body feels sculpted from ice. Even inside the car my feet are gelid.

I turn the key in the ignition, start the engine, fasten my seat belt, blast hot air from the heater, and turn the headlights on. Through the windscreen, I stare at the house I have just left.

A well-presented family home located just minutes from the motorway, providing easy access to the city and the south. This property boasts many features including an extended kitchen/dining/family room overlooking the private landscaped rear garden plus the added benefit of extra accommodation on the top floor.

Whenever a **FOR SALE** sign goes up on a property in the estate, my husband is thrilled at how much our 'asset' has accrued. But the house, in the beam of the headlights, looks more like a child's drawing than an asset, with sad window eyes and a door like a gaping mouth.

I engage the clutch, put the car in gear, depress the accelerator, and reverse out of the driveway, departing the estate through the two granite pillars designed to give a vestige of 'tradition' to the entrance. At the junction where I always turn right towards the city, I hesitate. The ticking of the indicator grows louder and the car behind flashes its lights. There is a strange, protracted moment of inertia, like a gap in time, then a sudden pump of adrenaline as I hit the indicator, make a sharp left instead.

The sky on the horizon is still dark. The clock on the dashboard reads 7:32.

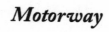

Motorway

Beyond the estate, the traffic slows on the link road and I pass cranes and cones, half-built office blocks and brand-new apartment blocks, before heading south. The motorway in the opposite direction is already transforming into a stagnant metal river. My lips feel dry and papery.

In the side mirror, a line of red tail-lights snake all the way back to the house where three people are still sleeping: my son, my daughter, my husband.

But I don't want to think about them now.

The sky is full of November white, more absence than colour, and along the motorway giant pylons flash silver. Control over speed, heat and sound induces a state of temporary calm, like standby, and scenery passes by in a stream of grey and green without me noticing it, as if there is a time delay; an image registers in my brain minutes after I have passed something: a new flyover under construction with abutments in place, a council crew spraying weedkiller and strimming grass, a layby with a sign saying **THIS AREA IS NOT A TOILET**, a lone beech tree in a field. I read somewhere that 20 per cent of American meals are eaten in cars. It doesn't surprise me. There is a peculiar pleasure in being insulated from the world while moving through it, especially in this luxury sport utility vehicle, a present from my husband for my fiftieth birthday, two years ago.

My husband, Tom: fifty-four, naturally thin, floppy grey hair, rumpled clothes, glasses, old leather satchel, runs his own media company. Prone to walking around the house saying, *Did you see my . . . ? Where is my . . . ?* Also, when I cook something, *From scratch?* A man who likes order and routine, whose taste in books, music, film was fully formed by his early twenties and has not changed since. Unlike his politics. To other women, 'an interesting man'.

With one hand on the steering wheel, I send him a text.

    —Work thing. Had to leave early. x

He took enormous pleasure in buying me the car and still gets a kick out of asking, *How's the motor running?* I was expecting a piece of jewellery or a handbag, but I like this car more than I admit. From inside it, the world is always slightly unreal. Sometimes I leave the house saying that I need to run an errand, but I just drive around instead. I like the sense of being nowhere, exactly. It's easier to think. I park in a quiet cul-de-sac and scroll through my phone, or I pick up a coffee and listen to the radio. It's never the same with a passenger on board. In the mornings, when my son gets out at his school, I love when I am alone again.

Fog clouds the motorway. I can see close up, but there is no depth of vision. Fields trees hedges, all washed out, disappear in mist. Then, just as suddenly, it lifts and pins of rain hit the windscreen.

My phone pings. A WhatsApp message from my son.

    —where you
    With one hand on the steering wheel, I message back.
    —Had to leave early for work.

I do not add *x*. He'll be annoyed I'm not there to drop him to school. I check the time. He can easily make the bus, if he hurries.

In the attic, my daughter will be stirring. She likes plenty of time to get ready for college.

My husband is still fast asleep in the master bedroom. In forty-three minutes, when the radar alarm goes off on his watch, he'll jump into the shower. It's a matter of pride with him, that he has engineered his days to avoid the worst of the traffic.

There is less than twenty minutes until my first class begins. It is policy to phone the school secretary if you are going to be absent, but the effort to put on the voice of the woman who is good at telling lies is too much this morning.

On the hills, black silhouettes of trees are lined up like sentries.

In the distance a young woman is standing beside a hatch-back that has its emergency lights flashing. I indicate, pull in and cruise up the hard shoulder towards her. She is platinum blonde, wearing runners as white as her teeth, and her hatch-back is new. She is squinting now, unsure whether to smile. I lower the window and unseasonably warm air shoots in.

—Are you OK?
—Ran out of petrol.
—Do you want a lift somewhere?
—Nah. My dad phoned the AA. They'll be here soon.
—Do you want me to wait with—
—No . . .

I bang the indicator and pull back onto the motorway. In the rear-view mirror, she is back on her phone. I imagine the message:

—*Weird woman just tried to get me into her car* 😶

13

The wipers are dragging on the windscreen. I hadn't noticed the rain stopping. Or the red low-fuel warning light.

The AA van passes on the other side of the motorway. Funny that we have the same word – *breakdown* – for mechanical objects and humans.

On the horizon there's a filament of white light.

I root in my handbag for ChapStick, but there is too much stuff in there to find anything.

Up ahead there is a large brown motorway sign. Stick figures of a man and woman. Crossed knife and fork. Cup and saucer. Petrol tank. Bed.

**TIREDNESS KILLS
TAKE A BREAK**

At the service station, the fuel cap is tight and the metal gun, when I lift it from the holster, is cold and heavy. A white van is parked on the forecourt with its engine running. Two men are inside. The older one stares at me while I fill the car, pretending to concentrate on the cascading numbers on the pump. When I check again, he is still staring, not a in a sexual way, but the way you might stare at an animal in the zoo. The gun clicks and I return it to the holster, tighten the fuel cap. He is still staring. I walk to the van, rap on the window. He rolls it down. He is in his sixties and wearing blue overalls.

—Hi. Do you know me?

He is confused. Beside him the younger man lets out a snort.
—No.
—Because the way you're staring, I thought you must know me.

His face darkens.

I cross the concrete forecourt braced for the sound of footsteps or a door slamming but I hear nothing. My lungs are airless.

Inside the service station, the attendant has one end of an exaggeratedly long scarf over his shoulder, the other end almost covering his mouth. I have to ask him to repeat his question.

—Pump number?

I look out. The white van is gone. I imagine the older man saying: *What a cunt.* And the younger man agreeing.

—Number 5.

I take cash from my wallet, then change my mind, take a card and insert it in the machine. My hand is shaking. Last year I set up an online account in my 'maiden' name, and this is the first time I have used the card the bank issued. I am not certain of the numbers. The woman behind me lets out a sigh.

—You can enter your PIN now.

I tap numbers on the pad. There is a pause, then an electronic clicking sound and the attendant's voice.

—Next!

The toilet sign is prominent.

MALE AND FEMALE OPERATIVES ATTEND TO THESE FACILITIES

In the ♀ a male operative is restocking the toilet paper dispensers with jumbo-size rolls. He is Asian, about thirty. In a cubicle, I sit to the side of the bowl to muffle the sound. After last night's wine, my urine is dark yellow. Back outside, in the mirror, a well-maintained woman from the suburbs stares back at me. I shake out my hair to see if the male operative notices, but he is busy mopping out a stall.

The service station is vast and has a factory-style roof. Beside the toilets truckers tap screens and wait in line for their numbers to be called. I spot a café in the distance.

Ahead of me in the queue for coffee is a businessman collecting a flat white, and two teenage girls ordering hot chocolate made with almond milk, no cream, extra marshmallows.

The woman on the till is pretty, green eyes and a ponytail. Her bump swells her uniform.

—What can I get you today?

Her accent is Eastern European.
    —Americano.
    —Any cakes with that?
    —No, just milk.
    —Do you have a loyalty card?
    —No.
    —Would you like a loyalty card? Or you can download the app to your phone.
    —No.

I pay with my new card, tapping it this time, and take my Americano to the seating area.

Through the window my car is holding up a pump.

On the wall there are black-and-white photographs of coffee beans spilling from hessian sacks and a sign. **SUSTAINABLE FAIR ORGANIC**. I clear used paper cups, a holder like a giant egg-box, nine napkins and two cardboard envelopes containing crusts from a table and sit down. In my handbag I find a packet of painkillers, burst two from their plastic capsules, swallow them with coffee. Then I take out eleven loyalty cards from my wallet, including one for this franchise and bend them back and forth until the plastic turns white.

On my phone, there are two new emails in the inbox, both work-related, and one in Junk. And a ribbon of newsfeed: Fires in Australia. Royal gets engaged. Undercover footage at farm in France shows deplorable conditions for pigs . . .

I tap the pencil symbol.

New Message

I type my work address.

Subject: Absence
I will be absent today due to illness.

I sign off, press Send, close off the app.

Nearby is a vending machine for toys in plastic balls, a display of tree-shaped car fresheners, a stand of Road Safety leaflets and a rack of Mermaid Room Signs.

> Freya's Room
> Grace's Room
> Hannah's Room
> Holly's Room

I scan down to my daughter's name.

> Lauren's Room

Beside this rack, another one of Superhero Room Signs.

> Fred's Room
> Harry's Room
> The slot for Mark's Room is empty.

SALE OF ALCOHOL PROHIBITED
UNTIL 10.30 A.M.

The back wall of the service station's grocery section is stacked high with booze. It is the kind of place that is perfect for picking up a bottle of wine with milk or cornflakes or a bag of apples, making it look like an afterthought. It is another part of my strategy of 'keeping a lid on things', to buy a single bottle of wine most days, rather than keeping it in the house. The final elements of my strategy included drinking between only six and nine on weekdays, hiding the open bottle under the sink with the wash-up liquid, and recycling regularly at some out-of-the-way bank where no one knows me.

My husband knows nothing about my strategy. He is the kind of drinker who *enjoys* Dry January. Do my children suspect anything? Probably not.

But they do know that some part of me is always elsewhere.

Outside, the day has fully broken. I ignore the cold stares of drivers queued behind my car, one of whom honks their horn, and depart past razed landscape, a hedge of denuded trees, a damp wooden picnic area with a sign.

GOODS LEFT AT OWNERS RISK.

There is no apostrophe on **OWNERS**.

Driving along the motorway that morning, my thoughts came loose, as if they had been stuck in a box that had suddenly opened.

At the service station, when I found my daughter's name in the rack of Room Signs, I felt queasy. I knew I would have bought it for her as a child. That for me, being a mother consisted of buying things for her. A lifetime of polyethylene before they were three.

My daughter, Lauren: almost twenty-one, petite, pretty, studying Drama and English at university. I had started to dislike her, or dislike her type: young women who live at home in converted attics with en-suite bathrooms, who have credit cards and Instagram accounts, boyfriends and girlfriends, veganism and feminism and the power to decide who is a creep and who isn't, who is a bitch and who isn't. Young women who fly on airplanes but go crazy if someone forgets to recycle a yogurt tub, who blame everything on their parents' generation and cry if they see a dead fox on the road.

I remember the feeling I had of being connected to my body when I was pregnant with Lauren, to all bodies, to trees, to birds in the sky, to the Earth turning on its axis; when Tom and I were as happy as children, sleeping and eating and playing house, all the while pent with expectation.

But even before Lauren was born, the feeling faded, the PURCHASING began. A crib. A changing table. A rocking chair. A baby monitor. Linen. Bottles. Bibs. A steriliser. A high chair. Bowls. Spoons. Jars of organic food. Nappies.

Cream. Talcum powder. Towels. A thermometer. A baby bath. Indoor clothes. Outdoor clothes. Hats. Sleepwear. A snowsuit with bunny ears. A stroller. Blankets. A car seat. A swing. Soft toys. Teething ointment.

And it never stopped. Crèche fees, school fees, extracurricular-activity fees, birthday parties, presents, Disneyland, Lapland, grind fees, fees for trips to ski in Switzerland, college fees, phones, game consoles, laptops, branded runners, cars.

And it never ended.

I lost that simple joy I had when I was pregnant. Or I allowed myself to lose it. All I remember of being pregnant with Mark is wanting to get it 'done'. I didn't even attend the antenatal classes.

Why is it that every class attended by women, from antenatal to Zumba, has someone at the top of the room shouting:

—Come on, girls!

Along the motorway weak sunshine flickers for a while. And then, as if someone has turned a dimmer switch, the day darkens and rain hits the windscreen again. A dead fox is lying in the grass median strip. A young one, by the look of it. Short fur, no trace of blood.

Beyond the last reaches of the city, farmhouses squat in square yards surrounded by rectangular fields, most of them empty, some with cattle or sheep.

The car is floating now, as if of its own free will. Motorways are the perfect form: lines with end stops of 'arrival' shimmering in the distance, the great illusion of progress.

Large blue signs loom on the motorway at decreasing intervals.

ROSSLARE EUROPORT

And then signs for Arklow, the seaside town where I grew up.

30 KM
10 KM
NEXT EXIT 2 KM

Something in me bends towards the past or childhood or what is familiar, and my hands, on the steering wheel, develop a faint tingling sensation. I keep straight on, in the inside lane, slowing and then accelerating, and slowing again, until, at the last moment, I hit the indicator, drift down the slip road.

Trees disappear, then bushes, then other cars, and, for a moment, everything is quiet before it is loud again.

I have not been back to this town for years. Not since we moved my mother into a nursing home in Dublin and sold the family home. It was an old council house and my brother and I couldn't believe how much it made, but it all went in nursing home fees and medical expenses. Well, nearly all. When she died last spring there was a small amount left in her account but I said nothing about it, either to my husband or to my brother in Australia. I just transferred it to a Revolut account that I opened in my 'maiden' name.

The outskirts are the same as those of every other small town in Ireland: a retail park, a stretch of car dealerships, middle-class housing estates with manicured entrances, a newbuild school, horses grazing on land zoned years ago for development. Nearer the centre there are more familiar landmarks. The once-stately terrace where my best friend lived and a Masonic Hall with a Tesco Express grafted onto its side.

Arklow was once a thriving town. There was a large pottery plant, where my father worked, and a munitions factory and a huge chemical fertiliser plant. They had closed, one after the other, leaving unemployment and a high suicide rate.

Now, all the signs are for a new shopping centre. I open the sat-nav, check the name on the signs, and dictate:

—Riverside Shopping Centre.
—*At the next roundabout bear left for Riverside Shopping Centre ... bear left ... in 1km at the roundabout ... bear left ... 200m ...*

Approaching it, the traffic thickens and I get glimpses of other drivers biting their nails or talking into phones, food wrappers scattered on passenger seats. I experience the same mild distaste at service stations when I feel myself unpeeling from the warm car seat to fill the tank, like a prawn emerging from a shell.

On the footpath, a man with a chiselled face is walking a greyhound. Two women in pink T-shirts power past him, **BREAST CANCER** bobbing up and down on their chests.

Further on, a teenage boy waits for a bus with a schoolbag at his feet. Litter has massed inside the shelter. Cans and crisp bags, sweet papers, a plastic bag.

The day hangs in the balance between weak sunshine and grey clouds.

—*You have reached your destination.*

The new shopping centre is impressive, a huge steel-and-glass edifice with a vast wraparound apron. At the barrier to the car park, the image on a grainy black-and-white video screen is of a blonde woman in a houndstooth coat. When the barrier shunts up I drive to the top level to get a view. Only two other vehicles are parked here – a station wagon near the entrance and an old beat-up jeep in the corner.

At the metal railings I button my coat against the wind. The coastline is ghostly, boundaries blurred between sea and sky, and, in the distance, the old pottery plant where a girl was murdered years ago. The facade has fallen into ruin, but the shell is still intact. Concrete does not decay. In the opposite direction, the large Catholic church where my mother took us to Mass, and behind it the council estate where we lived. In the opposite direction, the secondary school where I met my best friend, Elaine. From this vantage point the town is completely still, the only movement is the flow of the river.

The wind is agitating my hair again and my handbag tugs heavily on the sleeve of my coat. I bought this bag on a shopping trip to New York with Elaine – cocktails for breakfast and nightclubs and lines of cocaine – the year before she met her husband. The leather is worn, but the monogram is still bright.

Beneath the metal railing is a long strip of thin grey road.

A ringtone. Work, I presume. I should be in class by now teaching third years. But it's my daughter's name on the screen: *Lauren calling*. She never calls. She always messages.

It must be an emergency. My whole body freezes.

It rings out.

I wait for the symbol that indicates voicemail. I wait and wait, and then like an electric shock, my phone rings again. Her name on the screen again. I press the SILENT button. If it is an emergency she will leave a voicemail or message.

Yesterday afternoon, when I arrived home from work, a baby-blue Fiat 500 was blocking the driveway. In the house there was a bad smell. Lauren's cat had used the living room as a litter tray. I sent a WhatsApp message to the attic.

—*Can you come down here please?*
No response. And then, as I was about to press CALL, a creak on the floorboards. Minutes later she appeared in the kitchen, hair tousled, still in pyjamas.
—What?
—Can you please ask your friend not to block the drive-way? And why are you not at college?
—I'm on a reading week. Jesus. What's bugging you?
She took an apple from the fruit bowl and was gone. Me yelling after her:
—LET YOUR FUCKING CAT OUT.

I put my hand to my chin, detect a nascent bristle. And I need the toilet again. Above my groin, the service station coffee has pooled uncomfortably.

Nearing the entrance to the shopping centre, I realise that a man has been sitting in the driver's seat of the station wagon the whole time, watching me. He is about fifty, and wearing tinted glasses.

I slow to a stop, stare at him until he looks away.

Inside the automatic doors, Christmas muzak is playing over the PA system. The tiled lobby is empty except for a claw crane stuffed with soft toys and a parking ticket machine.

CHANGE IS POSSIBLE is written on the ticket machine.

In Japan so many people disappear that they have a word for them – *Johatsu*. It refers to 'evaporated people'.

But I had not evaporated.

It was early December – nearly three weeks since I had left the house in the suburbs – when the police traced me to a cottage in Wales. The male officer (older, white) did the questioning while the female officer (younger, black) darted her eyes around for any signs that I was not 'in my right mind'.

Two days later my husband turned up. Hearing his Merc outside, I felt a dying butterfly flapping in my stomach. He could not disguise his shock at my appearance – I was wearing a man's jumper and my hands were black from lighting the fire – and I caught the flicker of horror in his eyes at my short hair, already greying at the roots.

We spent the rest of that day talking and not talking while I drank half the bottle of whiskey he had brought in from the boot of his car: a single malt in a wooden box some client had given him. He sipped the same glass, constantly topping it up with water. He told me that when I hadn't returned home, he had gone to the Guards to report me missing. But they had very little interest in Absent-Without-Leave mothers from the suburbs and he'd had to threaten litigation to get them involved. I said mothers from the suburbs must take more road trips than we think, but he didn't find this funny.

What he wanted to know was WHY? Why would a woman get up one morning, leave her job, home, husband and children, and never come back? I had no idea what to say so I told him that things had been mounting up for a long time. He looked at me with disbelief, then contempt.

—Like what?
I had no answer.

Around midnight, it got very cold. I had let the fire die and there was no extra bedding for the sofa so we ended up both sleeping in my bed. There was a moment, in the early hours, when our bodies nearly had sex before our brains remembered the situation. Some sort of baggage reclaim instinct.

The next morning my husband was all business. *Affairs to be sorted out . . . our affairs . . . your affairs.* He said the word so often I thought it might be a Freudian slip. And he repeatedly alluded – in a tone that suggested I would have no idea of this place – to the *real* world. Watching his lips move in the tight musculature of his face, I thought he also looked older. Still handsome, still an interesting man, but older. His shirt was ironed and his tan corduroy trousers were new, but his eyes, which I had always thought his best feature, looked more steel than grey in daylight.

Then things got ugly.

—What about your CHILDREN? Can you not FOR ONE FUCKING MINUTE think about them?

I tried to point out that, strictly speaking, at eighteen and nearly twenty-one, they were no longer children.

That was a mistake.

—Can you not think about *anyone* but yourself . . . consider *their* needs, what *they* might be going through while you are off *finding* yourself. Lauren hasn't eaten a thing in weeks, not a thing, and Mark's grades are falling ... I had to go to the school and explain that his mother ... it was humiliating ...

I had never seen my husband so angry. For a moment I thought he might hit me. For a moment, I wanted him to hit me, to break everything, that whole *unreal* world that we had been so busy constructing, brick by brick, following some invisible blueprint – jobs, cars, house, kids, attic conversion, holidays in France – all the while ignoring that the forests were burning and the seas were rising and the soil was full of pollutants, deluding ourselves that there was some great dome that could be put over middle-class housing estates in Dublin to keep our children safe. With all our *correct* parenting, I told him, we had failed to teach our children a single skill – how to fish or sew or cook, how to bind a wound or light a fire.

And we were going to pat ourselves on the back for that?

He stomped out of the cottage, banging the door so hard that the glass rattled, and drove away at speed.

I started to laugh. And I couldn't stop. *Fishing* and *sewing*. Where had that come from? I fell back on the couch, almost hysterical ...

But the thing is, my father could fish, my mother could sew.

Weeks later, I made a list. Because what I had said to my husband was true. For years, things *had* mounted up: in drawers, racks, presses, the utility room, the shed, in the hot press, in the glove compartment of the car, under beds, at the back of closets, the bottom of old make-up bags and in recycling bins, in the back of my mind, in the arteries of my heart ...

Laundry.

Coupons, shopping bags.

Old make-up tubes and powder compacts.

Near-empty glass perfume bottles, plastic shampoo bottles, plastic shower gel bottles.

Necklaces, scarves, bags, belts, bracelets, rings.

Bedlinen, bath towels, tea towels, duvets, picnic blankets.

CDs, DVDs, memory sticks, external hard drives, game consoles.

Bikinis, flip-flops, sunglasses, sarongs, straw hats, almost-full sun creams.

Spices past their best-before-date.

Pens, pencils, markers, unused diaries.

Sports gear that no one ever used.

Broken terracotta pots, old camping equipment.

Empty wine bottles.

Photographs, so many photographs.

Batteries, old mobile phones, old mobile phone chargers, HDMI cables.

Single earrings, single socks, single gloves.

ChapSticks, lipsticks, tins of Vaseline.

Faces of students whose names I could no longer remember.

Jumbled impressions of cities I had visited.

Text messages, email threads, WhatsApp messages.

Dreams, fantasies, free-floating anxiety, anger with no obvious target.

Unread books, unseen films, unheard music.

Conversations I had never had.

Desire I had never felt.

Love I had lost.

Shopping Centre

While I'm in the lift to the Main Shopping Hall, my phone pings. A WhatsApp message from Lauren. I am flooded with relief as I open it.

—*Tried phoning but you obvs busy. Offer ends midday.* 🎄 *https://www.fittones.com/global/us/products/smartwatches/versa*

I tap the link and a page opens advertising an expensive watch to track steps, calories, blood pressure, etc.

I remember holding her at dawn in those first weeks of her life, the way the light fell, the chill, the scent of winter with its intimations of death, the warmth of her tiny body, sucking in rhythm, satisfying itself so completely.

I unbutton my coat. I am too hot and the black trousers are cutting at the crotch. The underwire of my push-up bra is digging into my ribs and, inside the ankle boots, my toes are pinched, my shins itchy from pop socks.

The Main Shopping Hall consists of franchise stores, a vape stand, kiddie rides, a hair salon, a coffee shop, a pharmacy, a FOOD HALL, and empty units trying to disguise their plight with facades. The same as every other shopping centre.

At the entrance to the anchor supermarket there are tubs of Christmas sweets stacked to the ceiling, alongside a wicker basket of cut-price pumpkins. Behind them, an enormous poster of a 'happy family' opening presents around a decorated tree.

A woman approaches holding a phone in front of her like it is a microphone.

—Yup . . . exactly.

She sits down on the bench beside me.

—I think she deserves everything she gets. I mean, dating sites, at her age . . . OK . . . well, keep me posted. No . . . God forbid . . . [laughter] . . . Can you imagine? [more laughter] . . . I know . . . I know . . . what next?

She stands up, adjusts her handbag, smooths her puffer jacket, and smiles conspiratorially at me. To her, I am another middle-aged woman with nothing better to do than roam the shops for early Christmas presents on a Tuesday morning in November.

I shrug my shoulders at her.

She recoils, disappears in the direction of the FOOD HALL.

In the American-style diner, a former student is behind the counter wearing a soda jerk cap and an apron. I cannot believe it. They turn up everywhere.

He is of average height, with bleached hair, carrying some weight since I last saw him. I try to retrieve his file from memory – *lazy, pleasant, no interest in art* – but I cannot recall his name. And then I see his name tag: Finn.

—Hey, Miss?
—Hi.

I do not smile or make small talk.

YOU'LL NEVER MISS BREAKFAST AGAIN

Reading from the poster above Finn's head, I order American Pancakes with Maple Syrup and a large Americano.

While he relays the coffee order to his co-worker, removes pancakes from a cellophane wrapper and places them in a toaster, assembles plastic cutlery, paper napkins and condiments on a tray, I run through my head the exchange that we might have had:

[Smile]
—Hi! How are you Finn?
—Yeah, good! Finished college last year. Just working here while I find a job.
[Keep smiling]
—Great!
—Yeah. Went travelling this summer. Thailand. Vietnam . . .

—Sounds brilliant! Well, nice seeing you. Good luck with everything.

[Even bigger smile]

But I am sick of being a 'teacher' at all times.

Only eight more years to retirement, I remind myself, but this morning it depresses rather than cheers me.

Finn drops a pancake on the floor, and has to start again.

I take a seat by the window. Behind me someone has chalked on a blackboard. *You can't buy happiness, but you can buy a Spiced Pumpkin Latte!* The apostrophe is correctly placed.

The pancakes come with Golden instead of Maple Syrup. I peel back the foil, dribble it over them anyway.

A WhatsApp message from Mark.

I open it:

> —*left gym bag at home can you drop it later*
> No salutation. No apostrophe. No question mark.
> I fire back:
> —*I am in work*
> There is no reply. Not even an emoji.

I sip the Americano, waiting for my pulse to slow.

My last class the day before had been Sixth Year Art History.

—Listen up, people!

I had forgotten to photocopy the handout on the Impressionists and had to wing it. My voice sounded thin and distant, as though not enough oxygen could get to my lungs. And the students were not listening. They were chatting or asking to go to the toilet or sending messages on phones stashed inside pencil cases. What they were interested in was collecting the handout and learning it by rote for the examination, since they had already signed in and gained the attendance credit. A few were not shy in communicating this. I tried to spark the old electricity that had earned me the reputation of being a good teacher – taking off my jacket and moving around, making big body language – but it was like trying to light a match in the rain.

—Are we getting our essays back?
—Next class.

I put a DVD on, turned off the lights.

They were soon half-asleep. Was it really only yesterday? I glanced at the time on my phone. I should be in class now teaching first years how to make a colour wheel.

I had wanted to be an artist, not a teacher.

The Story of How a Woman Becomes a Teacher and Not an Artist is an old one.

You have probably heard it many times.

There is only one version.

It goes like this.

The woman is busy making art, but all around her are the stories from real life – of money, of love, of babies – and the woman starts to listen to these stories. Every time she is forced to decide, she makes the easier choice. Postponement. She will return to making Art as soon as she has a reliable source of income and/or when she is married and/or once her children are older. In the meantime, the woman will 'stay in touch' with Art by teaching it, congratulate herself on this perfect solution, and avoid ever having to admit, especially to herself, that the thing she claimed to love so much, she didn't love that much, after all.

I did try, once, to change.

In my mid-forties, I took a 'career break', while actually intending never to return to teaching. Our children were older and my husband's company had taken off. It was an exciting time. After school, college, job, marriage, house, children, here I finally was with choices.

I joined a collective of painters and sculptors, mostly women, who had exhibition space and studios in a state-owned house. There were designated time slots for access to the studios, and at first everything was amazing. But after a few months of drinking coffee and sketching in a notebook, I realised that I didn't know what I was doing. I'd get the genesis of an idea, but I could never stay with it long enough to allow it to develop into anything real. I made a few sculptures, some of them well-received, but by the end I was secretly happy to succumb to the demands on my time. Either Mark had a football match or Lauren had rehearsals or the cat needed to be taken to the vet. And Tom was always busy.

I could talk about what I was trying to do. For hours. Especially over a glass of wine.

—My work at the moment . . .
—Confronts gender inequality . . .
—Repackaging the mundane . . .
—The piece I am currently working on . . .

When I thought of myself as an artist, it was in images borrowed from television and the internet, from books and magazines. Converted stone outhouses with canvases sprawled everywhere, an open bottle of wine on a trestle table, a cat lying in the sun.

But the reality was emails about 'kitty money' and 'Fairtrade' tea and water damage to the pottery kiln caused by whoever had left the window open the previous Monday.

After two years, I returned to teaching.

My husband said nothing, he had liked the idea of having an 'artist wife'. But my mother was more practical. *It would be mad to leave without the pension.*

Beyond the window of the diner, there is a communal area with benches, tubs of obedient trees, and a boardwalk along the river. This 'rejuvenation' plan must have looked great on a display board, with multi-ethnic figures relaxing in sunshine, but in the real world of a depressed seaside town a few vaguely menacing teenagers are hanging around the boardwalk, smoking a spliff, and a young mother in a thin zip-up is scrolling her phone while her toddler strains to get out of its buggy.

Outside the confines of the landscaped area, litter has bandaged to brambles and waste has been dumped inside metal railings, including the polystyrene inside of a car seat.

At a staff meeting recently, a booklet with the title **STUDENT INFORMATION CONFIDENTIAL** was handed out. The students' names were in one column and their special educational need and/or disability and/or mental health issue in another. I flicked through the pages, noticing that there were only a handful of students with a blank space beside their name. An entire generation were struggling, it occurred to me, and no one was asking WHY. The principal was jabbering away about child protection and mandatory reporting.

But no one was listening.

My Americano has gone cold.

Finn half-waves goodbye as I leave.

Further up the concourse, I push against the heavy glass door of a hair salon.

—Can I help you?

The young receptionist is trying to look like a mannequin. On her desk a vase of flowers with large waxy petals, and a reed diffuser.

—I want to get a blow-dry.
—Do you have an appointment?
—No.

Pink shellac nails flutter across a keyboard.

—Mandy is free.

The receptionist leaves, returns with a hairdresser.

—Hi, I'm Mandy.

She takes my coat, hangs it up.

—Would you like to come with me?

Mandy is plump, in her late thirties. Beige make-up and a chiffon blouse over ill-fitting trousers. Her accent is local, flattened vowels and soft consonants, and it strikes me that I must have had this accent once.

On the leather couch, she fluffs my hair and, asks what I am thinking of having 'done'. Something in me kicks, and I tell her that I want it cut shorter.

—A bit shorter?

—No. Much shorter.

At the basin, she turns on the water.

—Is this temperature all right for you?

The water is tepid and there is a mechanical cat purring on my back. The massage setting on the chair has been activated. Nails graze my scalp. I close my eyes until there is only the sound of water and female voices, the sudden explosion of machines, a smell of coconut and body odour.

—If you'd like to come with me.

The final journey to the mirror.

—Coffee? Tea? Water?
—No.
—Magazines?
—Yes.

Mandy rifles through a stack of magazines, dismissing the trashier ones, selecting more upmarket publications for me. I flick through one as she starts to snip. It is full of cosmetic smiles and photoshopped bodies, ads for Korean Silk Handmade Eyelashes and labia-plasty, an article on 'How To Survive The Menopause'.

At the edge of my vision, strands of hair are falling to the floor. Then a pause in the snipping. Mandy is losing her nerve.

I encourage her.

—A bit more off.
—Just to here?
—A bit shorter than that.
—Just to here?

I give up.

Tics of exhaustion are breaking through Mandy's practised friendliness.

Around me, women are getting their hair 'done'.

They sit in tin foil and gowns, under dryers and wrapped in towels, tapping and scrolling screens, making and taking calls, drinking coffee, reading magazines.

How women love getting things 'done'. Hair, housework, dinner, ironing, gardens, home extensions, nails, family portraits, attic conversions, sex, pregnancy, Christmas shopping.

Before she went into a nursing home, my mother spent a year sitting in a spotless house with *everything done*. You could hardly finish a cup of tea before the cup was in the dishwasher. She had replaced the open fire with gas, the carpet with laminate flooring, the upholstered couch with a leather one, the washing line with a dryer, the grass lawn with cobble loc. And she could not get enough of Meals-on-Wheels dinners that could be heated in the microwave and eaten straight out of the packaging.

—How's that?

When I look up, the contrast between the image in the mirror and those in the magazine, feels, for a split second, like a glitch.

—Fine.

Mandy switches on the blow dryer. By the time she switches it off, I am burning. Not just my scalp, but my whole body. My neck, where it emerges from my white shirt, is blotched.

45

—Hairspray?
—No.
—A little mousse?
—No.

Mandy looks deflated.

Almost involuntarily, words come out of my mouth.

—All set for Christmas?

The question pumps air into Mandy. Suddenly, she is alive again. She tells me she has three for Santa and slips her phone from her back pocket to show me her screen saver. Two boys and a baby wrapped in a pink blanket.

—That's Liam. He's seven. And that's Frankie. He's five. He's a character, I can tell you. You have to be up early for him. And that's Róisín. She's two now. The photo is from when I brought her home from hospital. She's an angel. The apple of her daddy's eye. Already knows how to twist him around her finger . . .

In the house I left this morning, there are framed black-and-white portraits on the wall beside the stairs. In them my husband and I, my daughter and my son, all wearing blue jeans and white T-shirts, are in our bare feet. In one photograph, we are lying on the floor laughing at a balloon. In another, we are holding hands and jumping in the air. In a third, we are bunched tightly together like a sports team. The studio session had taken four hours of poses and retakes, and had ended with a row in the car on the way home.

You will find such photographs, or versions of them, in many comfortable homes in the suburbs. They show that the family who live there are happy.

There is a change in the tone of Mandy's voice and I redirect my ear to what she is saying.

—Not myself after the second one. Thought for a while I was going to have a stint in the funny farm. But a few smarties, a bit of a rest, and sure I was grand again. You know how it is. Thank God nothing like that with the last one.

I watch her reflection in the mirror making the sign of the cross.

For a terrible moment, I think I'm going to tell Mandy that my mother died last year. I feel the words loosening, ready to make the journey up my throat and out of my mouth. But they are not real words. They are words born of a compulsion to speak.

I swallow hard, push them back down.

I do not want to talk about my mother. I do not want to talk at all. What I want is to be silent. Or else to have a conversation that does not revolve around my husband, my daughter, my son, my dead mother, my job or my house.

The receptionist appears and leans into Mandy's ear.

—Your next appointment.

And Mandy is all business now.

She shows me the back of my head in a hand mirror, unties the gown, sweeps dead hair from my shoulders, escorts me from the chair, and tells the receptionist at the desk what I've had 'done'.

I pay with my new card, leaving no tip.

On the leather couch, Mandy is smiling at a dour-looking woman in a purple anorak.

In the glass front of a retail outlet, I look like one of those pictures where someone draws the head and someone else draws the body. With my hair shorter, the clothes I am wearing are ridiculous. The houndstooth coat is stuffy and the costume brooch, in this amnesiac setting, screams 'teacher'.

Inside the outlet, it is busy. Women are spread out evenly over the floor space, rummaging through shelves, leafing along racks, pulling hangers apart, clacking them together again, shopping for themselves, their husbands, their children, their mothers, their husbands' mothers, friends, colleagues, teachers, neighbours. My eyes snag on items that usually interest me – a tomato-coloured corduroy jacket, an eco-friendly silk pillowcase – but I have no interest today.

What I want is clothes that do not look ridiculous with short hair.

I take a basket, pick out different sizes of denim jeans, a thermal vest, a cable-knit polo neck in sea green, a pair of runners, sports socks, a casual beige trench coat, a three-pack of cotton knickers, a sports bra.

While I am selecting a coat, a woman barrels along the rack presuming that when she reaches me, I will give way. I stop dead. She hesitates, moves on.

The girl on the desk at the FITTING ROOM has squirrel-tail eyebrows and is not paid enough to hide her boredom. She hands me a plastic disc for the jeans and takes my basket in case I steal anything.

In the changing room, there is a narrow shelf and two pegs for hanging clothes. I try the middle-sized pair of jeans first. They are a bit loose, but they'll do. Inside my shapewear knickers, the panty liner has buckled.

The girl with the eyebrows takes the disc and reject jeans, hands me back my basket.

A long queue wends its way to the PAY POINT, past socks, tins of biscuits, scented candles, male grooming products, pet toys, stationary . . .

In front of me there is a couple. Retirement age. He is carrying a stack of bedlinen. She is consulting a list. They exchange sudden bursts of conversation.

I've always hated these couples whose marriages 'work' through shopping together.

I add a Silver Tone Fabulous Feet Toenail Cutter to my basket. And a tweezers.

—Till number six please.

A young guy locates the tag on each item, bleeps it, folds the clothes into large paper bags, using three in all. He has greasy hair and a bandage over his left earlobe.

He asks if I would like to donate €1 to charity.

—No.

I am not in the mood to play the game of 'good' shopping, for rich people, and 'bad' shopping, for the poor.

I take the escalator back up to the toilets, undress in a wheelchair-accessible cubicle, throw the buckled panty liner from my knickers in a bin that smells of stale blood, and use the toenail cutter to clip the labels from the new clothes before I put them on. Then I squash all my old clothes into a large paper bag and leave it beside the bin.

There are posters for a recycling scheme in the retail outlet, but I can't be bothered to **GIVE UP CLOTHES FOR GOOD.**

I glance at my reflection in a mirror. I look like an extra from a French film.

In the Hair Salon, part of me would have liked to boast to Mandy about my children. She would have been impressed. They are academically high-achieving, health-conscious, well adapted. I could have flashed up a photo on my phone, told her that Lauren was in UCD studying English and Drama – a bit of a diva – and that Mark played right wing on the rugby team at his prestigious all-boys school – where his father went before him.

OR

I could have told her about the time, when Lauren was about eight, and we had rented a gîte in France. It was the first year that Tom's business had made 'real' money. A couple he knew had come to visit us. Mr Nice & Mrs Gorgeous. The man was in the same 'game' as Tom, a useful contact, and the woman illustrated children's books. He was warm and funny and she was slim and pretty. But all weekend Lauren played up – splashing her brother in the pool, being cheeky, showing off – and by their last evening my mask of Good Wife/Mother/Hostess began to crack. The fourth time I had to return her to bed (after she had come downstairs while we were eating), I snapped. I pushed her into the bedroom, forced her down onto the bed and made breathless threats into her face until there was silence. Then I went to the bathroom, freshened my lipstick, returned to the living room, refilled everyone's glass (especially my own) and sat back on the couch.

OR

I could have told her about how my son transformed when he was fifteen, becoming obsessed with going to the gym, drinking protein shakes, earning a place on the school rugby team, doing well in exams. That this had come about following some 'prank' involving older boys on the rugby team. He had tried to tell me about it one day in the car, while we were running late for an orthodontist appointment. When he started sobbing uncontrollably beside me in the passenger seat, I panicked, reaching frantically for tissues in the glove compartment, almost rear-ending the car in front, and ending up in an argument with the other driver. The moment had passed. Later, I tried to bring up the subject again, suggesting he talk to the school guidance counsellor but it was too late. My husband was delighted with Mark's transformation. Only I saw the guarded look in his eye, the sneering grin.

My son Mark now: eighteen, tall, athletic, obsessive about going to the gym and rugby, intolerant of anyone with a worldview different to his own.

Calling him in the mornings always makes me feel like a barking dog:

—Mark Mark MARK!

Yesterday morning I lost patience and barged right into thick air and a hairy leg sticking out from under a Marvel duvet, the pillage of clothes, cans and wrappers, an empty pizza box.

—Mark Mark MARK! Get up. You'll be late for school—
It was quiet and breathy but I heard it . . . *bitch*.
—WHAT DID YOU SAY?
—Nothing, I'm up. Jesus. I'll be down in a minute.

I could hear my husband's voice in my head. *Just go to work and let him be late for school. How else will he learn personal responsibility?*

It was an argument we'd had a million times.

Mark, so soft-natured as a child that when we went for a walk in the park, he blew kisses to birds.

Sometimes, here in Wales, when I am cycling or walking to the village or travelling on the bus to town, I find myself trying to make a story out of what happened, as if I am lying on a couch talking to a psychiatrist. Another authorised version of events, if you like. Authorised by myself this time. But I can never work out exactly where to begin, or where to end. A story needs a beginning and an end, but in life there are no such things, only birth and death.

That last morning in the house in the suburbs, as I lay in bed listening to Tom breathing in the darkness, I was still certain, despite the despair that I had felt the previous night, that I loved my husband.

I had been sitting at the island in the kitchen, drinking a glass of wine and enjoying the solitude, when I heard the front door opening, keys dropping in a ceramic bowl. I corked the wine, put it in the corner cabinet.

—Anyone home?
—In here. I thought you had a work thing?
—Good news! Sealed the deal.

He plonked a bottle of champagne on the marble island.

—I'd have kept dinner if I'd known you'd be home.

This was a lie.

But he already had his back to me, rooting in the fridge.

—Any cheese?

I was about to say that there was some Gouda in the drawer when I was overcome by a thick despondency, close to despair. I apologised, saying I had a headache, and went upstairs to bed, taking the glass of wine with me.

The foundation myth of our relationship was that Tom was strong, steady, boring, and I was fun, creative, fragile. And that we complemented each other. Opposites attract, and all that. I believed this unquestioningly.

When his Merc pulled up in front of the cottage in Wales in early December, eighteen days after I had driven out of the driveway that Tuesday morning, part of me, a big part of me, was relieved. *The game was over*, I thought. I had been silly and now he had come to *rescue* me. Enough was enough.

But Tom had not come to rescue me. This was just the story I was still telling myself, the story that I had been telling myself for years, and that I continued to tell myself for a long time after he had left again to return to Ireland. It was a story I wanted to be true.

But it wasn't true.

My husband had come to *berate* me, not to rescue me.

On some level he still loved me, as I loved him. But the great love of my husband's life was actually 'the moral high ground'.

I was making a flower bed at the back of the cottage, planting bulbs in the first sun of March, three months after Tom's visit, when I finally realised this.

I had to sit down on the damp soil.

But what was *my* great love? Dependence? Replacing the father who had died when I was eleven?

If, instead of chastising me, Tom had hit me or even broken down, crying like a boy, then I'd have gone back with him to the house in the suburbs. No question. I'd have sat into the passenger seat of the Merc, clicked the seatbelt, and rewound the journey back over the Irish Sea, back down the motorway and back through the granite pillars of the estate, returning to the driveway as though it had all been a dream. Perhaps we would have stopped at a service station. While he filled the tank, I might have bought coffees and croissants for us to eat along the way, joking about it being like when we dated, letting the conversation turn serious then, about what needed to be different, about how things had to change: less drinking by me, less checking of activity app by him. Better parenting. Therapy. Maybe build a studio in the garden for my sculpture. Looking at his hands on the steering wheel, at his face in profile, I might have seen a man I could fall in love with again.

I wanted to call him back after we had argued about our children, after he had left, slamming the door behind him and driving away at speed, when I had finally stopped laughing about teaching sewing and fishing to Mark and Lauren. If I hadn't already disposed of my phone, I would have called him. *Please. I'll do anything. PLEASE don't leave me . . .*

Until he left, part of me had thought that it was all still a game.

I didn't get dressed for days afterwards, just slept and ate food out of cans – beans, soup, pears in syrup – and lay on the sofa. I thought about opening the bottle of wine in the press, but I was too frightened of what drink might do to me.

On the fourth day, I got up, had a shower, walked into the village and took a bus to town, where I went into a café and had the best carrot cake I had ever tasted.

Those first days after I arrived at the cottage in Wales, I woke every morning with the intention of returning to the house in the suburbs. Then a week or so went by. Then Tom visited. Then Christmas passed in a haze. And then somehow it was February.

And now it is November again and I am still here.

I have three hens. There used to be four, but one died.

I also grow vegetables.

I have a dog. A mongrel, short-legged and tough, with a strong jaw for killing rats.

I have a friend. Her name is Lena. I don't know if I would still be here if I hadn't met her.

Most of the time I am alone, however.

I am more aware of the colours of the sky, the smells of the earth, the birds in the morning and evening, the feeling of being alive.

But that is on some days.

On other days, I wake up with bad dreams stuck to me, like cobwebs. I am locked in a dark room with the fog of the past and the fog of the future and I have no control over when I will be released.

I am learning that it is OK to live like this. It is just the way time is, when you are not distracted from it.

An hour, a whole day, can go by in easy rhythmic thoughts. And then, without warning, my mood plummets. The trigger is sometimes obvious, a letter in the post from Tom's solicitor or the sight of schoolchildren in the village. Other times it comes out of nowhere, and I collapse in the middle of the afternoon wondering what the point is. Then the red clock on the mantelpiece strikes six and I get up, put coal on the fire, make something to eat.

I walk or cycle to the village most days. It is something to do and people here are friendly, but not particularly nosy. They say hello, goodbye, thank you, the odd exchange about the weather. It is easy to be reclusive in Wales.

My hair has grown and has more grey in it.

Also, I got a tan in the summer that still hasn't faded.

I pay the rent in cash every month.

When Huw, the landlord, calls to collect it, we talk about the cottage. He brings me things that he says he has no use for: chicken wire, a poker for the fire, a mongrel dog. I take an envelope from a drawer in the kitchen and hand it to him. I asked once why the rent was so cheap and he told me he had tried to sell the cottage, but there were complications with the leasehold. He added that it was not everyone's 'cup of tea'. He smiled when he said that and we both laughed.

The rent includes bills and the landlord collects the rubbish himself.

Town

I exit the shopping centre. I need some fresh air, but also I want to walk around the town, see if I recognise anything. It has started to rain again, and I have no umbrella. I don't care. I want to feel the drops on my skin.

It had been a long time since I existed like this, a body moving through time and space, without any definite purpose. Walking usually means exercise along a set route in a designated time slot. The novelty of drifting induces a low-grade anxiety, but I ignore it.

With my shorter hair, I no longer have a stable exterior image of myself, and I feel lighter wearing runners.

On the bridge, I pause to look at the river. A pair of swans in the distance are stately and radiant, but below me, in the murky water, the dark shuddering of fish, and a shopping trolley lying on its side.

Strung out along the steps down to the boardwalk, the detritus of illegal activity and the graffiti.

SAY NO TO AUSTERITY

For a moment, the rain stops and thin sunshine picks out mica schist in the granite stone of the bridge, creating a faint, illusory atmosphere of uplift before, just as suddenly, grey clouds retake the sky.

When I was young, I could not wait to get out of this town, and after I left for art college, I hardly ever came back. Once or twice a year. Christmas; my mother's birthday. And even that ended after I got married and was able to insist that she visit me. In my larger house.

—Spare some change?

A man is sitting on the pavement, sheets of cardboard underneath him. On his lap, a Jack Russell with a kerchief around its neck. A small girl with her hair in ribbons reaches out to pet the dog as she walks by. It licks her hand and she shrieks. Her mother tugs her away, then returns and drops a coin into the man's paper cup.

I don't stop but he thanks me anyway.

—God bless you lady.

It must be habit.

Tom never missed a chance to point out the idiocy of giving money to homeless people.

—It makes no sense. They'll just booze it or buy drugs. Give the money to a registered charity instead, then the problem might get sorted.

The town has changed since I was young, but it feels the same. An agglomeration of pubs, charity shops, bookies, churches, dark narrow side streets. Even the newer buildings seem to contain ghosts of older architecture. There is a residue of melancholy in the betting shops, angel shops, in the **CASH FOR GOLD** signs and the **CLOSING DOWN SALE** signs. And a new greyness that I don't remember.

In the window of the bank where my mother used to lodge father's pay cheque every week there is a poster of a young couple buying their first home. But even that looks faded.

The dark, pungent smell of a pub cellar seeps through a metal grid in the pavement. The pub is painted matt black and the name is in gilt lettering. **FOLEY'S BAR**. In the window, a collection of bodhráns and faded antiquarian books.

My phone pings. A WhatsApp message from my brother in Cape Town.

—Thought we'd arranged to Skype @ two your time today sis???

I have no idea which pub in the town my father drank in. He died when I was eleven and my brother was five.

His funeral was on a cold day in May. Outside the church, people in coats shook my hand, patted my brother's head, told us to be good for our mammy. And then life went on the same as before. What I missed was going for spins. My mother couldn't drive so the car sat out on the road until some travellers offered to take it away. I remember the concrete underneath was a shade lighter than the rest of the road.

A heavyset man passes close by me, shaking the metal grid over the cellar. I consider going into the pub, just to sit for a while and think, but it is not the 'done thing', even in the twenty-first century, for a Mother to be alone in a pub in the afternoon.

I push against the heavy door, step inside.

It has been a long time since I was in a 'traditional' pub like this, with floorboards and stained upholstery, a dado rail, embossed wallpaper and old advertisements for Jameson Irish Whiskey and Powers Irish Whiskey, photographs of local GAA teams, a mirror with **GUINNESS IS GOOD FOR YOU** written on it, and an open fireplace, the briquettes on the cusp of collapse.

But this is actually a new pub, disguised to look like an old one, with CCTV cameras and hollow brick walls and an enormous screen in one corner with horse racing on.

The old boys at the bar pay no attention as I place my order and find a table. A middle-aged woman with short hair is invisible.

The barman brings the pint first, sets it on a mat, and returns a few minutes later with a toasted sandwich, two sachets of mustard, cutlery rolled in a napkin. The cheese is warm and melds perfectly with the tarry, bitter Guinness.

It had also been a long time since I held a pint glass in my hand.

At the next table, an older couple are eating soup. They have an impassive look about them, as if they eat here every day. The smell is unappealing. Vegetables microwaved too hot.

I miss the grey cloak of cigarette smoke in pubs.

The weather app on my phone shows a cloud with raindrops falling from it, but beyond the pub window there is no rain.

Halfway through the Guinness, I decide that skipping work was a great idea. Some darkness at my core is unfurling and the endless, black whirring of the **TO DO** list is gone. After the stupid affray with White Van Man at the service station and the silly stand-off with Woman In A Hurry in the retail outlet, a sense of calm is returning.

I decide not to reply to my brother.

He had zero interest in our mother while she was alive and now he wants me to send him her wedding ring for his fiancée, photographs and letters, and 'family stories' for his wedding speech. He thinks I don't notice him dropping eye contact during the Skype calls to scan some other more interesting window of his computer.

What does he want me to say? Which particular 'family stories' does he want to hear?

That our mother lived for six years in the nursing home? That she was fine for a year or two, but then began to decline, and that by the last year she was prey to every illness going. That it was tiring. The biweekly visits. The phone calls to doctors/nurses/care assistants. The prolonged palliative care. The funeral arrangements. The five stages of grief. That in those final months, I was so busy waiting for it all to be 'done' that I forgot what death meant.

OR

That in the nursing home our mother spent her time going over her 'life story'? The one that began in childhood with her as the Put-Upon Saint, continued in adulthood with her as the Martyred Wife and then as the Tragic Widow, and ended in the retirement home with her as the Neglected Old Woman. That the 'scripting' of this story was demanding and took all her energy. That right up until the end she remained vigilant for any sign of resistance to her version of events. A yawn at the wrong moment and she would grimace, revert to making complaints about the Filipino care staff stealing from her or the male nurse giving her the wrong medication.

OR

That our mother had picked up from TV and magazines that it is acceptable – no, *necessary* – for women to tell the 'true' story of their lives? And maybe it is. But in the end there was no one to listen to my mother's story, other than me, and I didn't want to hear it. I didn't want to know what our father was like with drink in him or that he'd had an affair with a woman from Newry, and that this was why there was six years between my brother and myself.

OR

That I tried to interest her in other things – in nursing home gossip, in her grandchildren, in the plot lines of TV shows – but that it was no good? That she spent her last few years circling in on herself, losing the present in a story of the past, until, in the end, she told her 'life story' in an agitated whisper that only she could understand.

At a small table in a corner of the pub, a man in his late sixties is reading a paperback with a cracked spine. The cover is familiar.

The man's clothes are good quality, a tweed jacket, olive-green corduroy trousers, but he is painfully thin. He sits with one leg crossed over the other and his fingers, on the book cover, are nicotine stained. He is drinking a pint of Guinness.

He catches me staring at the book and smiles.

—Do you know it?
—Yes.

I had recognised the still from a film adaptation on the cover.

I look away, into the creamy head of my Guinness.

—Good, isn't it? he asks.
I raise my glass.
—It certainly is.

Immediately, I realise my mistake. He meant the book. But then he laughs, says the Guinness here *is* indeed excellent, and I am struck by the sensitive brown eyes in his narrow face.

—May I?

He is holding his pint of Guinness high in the air, as if he is about to embark on a voyage.

—I'm sorry?
—May I join you?
—Please do . . .

He drops into the seat opposite me, centres his pint on a beer mat, places a pack of cigarettes and a box of matches beside it, holds out his slim hand and introduces himself as Jonathan.

He has an easy manner and we talk comfortably about the weather, about the storm at sea the night before, about the town and how it has changed over the years, about pubs and recreation in the afternoon. He wonders, without asking, why I am drinking so early. When I tell him that I teach art in a school in Dublin, he is surprised.

—My deepest respect, he says. I don't know how you manage it. Funnily enough, I tried it myself once, years ago. A few hours a week in the all-boys' school. But they were animals. Only one thing on their minds.

But gradually, we drift away from this and hit upon depictions of the sea in art.

—No other Irish painter captures the sea like Jack B. Yeats, he says. The colour. The iron grey and roiling green. Always some threat that is so *Irish* . . .

He smiles, keeps his hand cupped around the pint glass on the table, waits for my response.

—And, I add, so . . . visceral.

I wish I hadn't used the word. It's so 'teacher'. I struggle to recover.

His eyes look straight at me, deep brown.

—Do you know the work of Nano Reid, by any chance, he asks. Very undervalued. Her seascapes are—
—O, my God, yes.

My voice is too loud and Soup Couple cast a glance as they leave.

With an almost invisible gesture to the bar, Jonathan orders two more pints. When they arrive, I ask if he is an artist.

—An artist? No. I've dabbled a bit. Oil paintings. Portraits. But no artist. I have a gallery on the main street. Seahorse Art Gallery. Do you know it?

I tell him that I don't.

—Over the fireplace stuff, mostly . . . But a *few* names.

He searches the inside pocket of his jacket for a business card, but can't find one.

—There's a website now. Quite good. But it hasn't been updated in a while.

I tell him that Nano Reid was a favourite of mine, while I was still in college.

—I had a lovely little oil on board by Nano Reid last year. *A Rough Sea.*

I tell him I don't know the work, that teaching does this to you, makes you lose touch with the artists you love.

There is a pause in the conversation and then he asks what brings me to the town. I tell him I'm on a road trip and he seems to like that. He mentions the train to Rosslare Europort, the ferries to Britain, France, Spain, how connected the town is to the rest of the world these days.

The second pint is making me disinhibited, and it is hard for me to resist flirting with him. It is a habit I have with men who I assume are gay, touching their sleeve when they speak, listening too intently. I ask if the town is more liberal since the referendum on gay marriage. A mistake. He recoils from the question, and for a while, we fall back on small talk.

Gay marriage is legal in Ireland now, in the twenty-first century, and gay couples walk the streets holding hands, even in depressed seaside towns. But while the art dealer is probably not 'in the closet', he is not 'out' either. I have met men like this before, older gay Irish men, able to have sexual encounters, but with too much damage done for them to have more lasting relationships. Men who grew up being called *nancy sissy poof fairy fag*. Men who were beaten in school and at home. Men with invisible wounds all over them.

71

When we relax back into easy conversation, he offers me a cigarette. I say I don't smoke and he takes the pack and matches from the table, goes out to the smoking area. He has left his book behind. *The Servant* by Robin Maugham.

I order two more pints at the bar. I don't want to be The Woman Who Has Drinks Bought for Her. At least not with this man.

Waiting for the Guinness to settle, I step into a dark alcove and follow a **TOILETS** sign through a door, beyond which a man is urinating against a tea-stained porcelain wall, cistern blocks melting blue in the gutter beneath. I back out, away from the acidic smell, and locate the Ladies. This is what two pints in the afternoon have always done for me. They send me through the wrong doors.

In the mirror in the Ladies, there is no sign of the well-maintained teacher from the suburbs, just a ragtag-looking woman with short hair and dilated pupils. A poster on the wall reads **ACCESSING ABORTION IN IRELAND TODAY**.

When the Art Dealer returns we quickly recover the familiarity we had built up and we are discussing the peculiar atmosphere of seaside towns when the barman places the fresh pints on the table.

The Art Dealer is suddenly flustered, almost upset. His eyes are alarmed. His right-hand flutters in the air, drops to his lap, hovers in the air again.

I try to pick up where we have left off.

—Have you ever been to Margate?

But he is distracted. The tone of his voice, when he responds, is uncertain. His sentences fractured.

—Yes, yes … Emin … More celebrity than … That bed thing … That was … No, I have never had the pleasure of Margate … Tate Gallery, there now I believe …

Should I not have ordered the drinks? Should I not have paid for them? Is he one of those men who get annoyed when women take the initiative?

Then I understand. He is a 'regular', the same as Soup Couple. Two pints every day after lunch and a conversation with a stranger when the occasion arises. A solitary whiskey in the evening. A life so finely balanced between function and despair that no variation to routine, such as a third pint in the afternoon, can be accommodated.

But we drink on. And he talks on.

—The Tate in London … now that's …

I lose track of the conversation. My own memories of London distract me and when I look up again, the Art Dealer is fishing a scarf from the pocket of his jacket. Something in his shoulders makes me think of a kite falling to the ground when the wind dies. Then he gets up, shakes my hand again and leaves slowly, with a heavy walk for such a thin man. His pint is finished, just a scrim of beige on the inside of the glass.

When I was nineteen, I took a journey similar to the one he had mentioned. From my home in the council estate to the railway station. From our seaside town to the North Wall in Dublin. From Holyhead to an abortion clinic in London. We didn't call it a ferry, back then, we called it *the boat*. And even though my mother sat beside me all the way, it is an episode that never made its way into the story of her life. What I remember most is how bored I was. I had a small backpack and not any kind of case, for appearances, and it was difficult to fit everything in – a change of clothes, a nightdress, a toiletries bag – there was no room for a book.

And the bleeding afterwards.

I remember how it went on for weeks.

The pub is almost empty. The barman is leaning on the counter, reading the newspaper. Taking a break before the evening crowd.

I think about finishing my pint, but it's gone flat, and I have a slight headache again. But no painkillers. They are in the boot of my car at the shopping centre. I check the clock behind the bar. Nearly time to drive back to the house in the suburbs.

My phone pings. A text message from my husband.

 —Home late. x

I reply.

 —👍

When I re-watch the footage of that morning now, I see a woman who is so full of rage that it is amazing she doesn't 'harm herself or others'. This was one of the questions the police put to me when they turned up at the cottage in Wales – *Did I have any thoughts of harming myself or others?* I wanted to ask them, *Who doesn't have such thoughts?* But I simply answered 'Yes'/'No', let them tick their box, and move on to the next missing person case.

What was going through my head at the service station and the car park and the retail outlet? Mostly, it was a matter of feelings rather than thoughts. They don't always match up. Thoughts often come after – sometimes a long time after – feelings. And what was I feeling? An accelerated heart rate, heaviness in my stomach, tiredness in my legs, a headache, intermittent explosions of rage. I had the *feeling* of something being wrong, of something having been wrong for a long time . . . and a panicked desire not to *know* what it was. Because if I knew what it was, I might have to change my life. The woman walking around in tight ankle boots and uncomfortable shapewear knickers, was not *thinking* anything. She was too busy trying to persuade herself that all she needed in order to *feel* better were a few hours to drink coffee, browse the shops, maybe get her hair done.

That Tuesday in November, sometime in the brief lull between Halloween being over and the drumroll to Christmas beginning, when I drove out of the driveway of my comfortable home in the suburbs of Dublin and never came back, I wasn't *imbalanced* and I wasn't looking for *MORE*.

I was simply thinking about the few hours ahead in which I was not going to answer anyone's questions or tune in to anyone's mood or solve anyone's problems. Not going to give a thought to whether or not my son's rugby gear was still in his gym bag or whether or not my daughter was eating enough protein or if my husband had remembered to book his car into the garage to have the wheels balanced for an upcoming NCT.

And maybe if I hadn't met Jonathan and recognised something of myself in his loneliness, then, maybe, I would have collected the car, sobered up, driven back along the motorway to the house in the suburbs, the heater on at my feet, the stereo blasting my favourite CD.

I try to live by routine here in the cottage in Wales. It saves thinking.

Most days, I walk or cycle to the village. There is a small supermarket, a post office, an animal supplies shop, and a pub, along with a school and a church. It is a forty-minute walk or a ten-minute cycle on an old bike I found in the shed. Most Tuesdays, I take the bus from the village to the nearest town. The journey is less than an hour and the bus is always half empty. The driver nods recognition, but nothing more.

In town, I take out money from the ATM, visit the library, maybe browse the charity shops. Then I usually have an Americano and a slice of carrot cake in the community café before picking up items that I can't get in the village.

With no household bill in my name, I couldn't get a lending card for the library in town. When I mentioned it to Lena, she gave me hers. She said she never used it.

If the librarians are suspicious, they don't show it.

I still have the bottle of wine that I bought the day I arrived here. I never opened it. I keep it in the press under the sink with the wash-up liquid and a lunchbox containing batteries and light bulbs and an old brass doorknob. The interior of the press is dark, the U-bend creating an odd-shaped space that attract spiders and dust. I don't drink alone anymore but like knowing the wine is there, in case of an emergency.

What else?

My hair has grown out but I no longer wear make-up. I am the woman in wellington boots and a rain jacket, my only accessory a mongrel dog. Without cosmetics and hair dye, I have aged, but not shockingly, and I am content with how I look.

In the spring I planted vegetables in the garden, carrots and potatoes, and some herbs and rhubarb. Next year I will try runner beans.

The worst time this year was in August when a rat burrowed under the wire and attacked one of the hens. I knew something was wrong when I went up the garden to collect the eggs. It was too quiet and three of the hens were huddled together at the back of the coop. I saw the other one lying on its side, twitching. Huw had warned me about rats. I carried the injured hen into the cottage, put it in the sink, and ran water until it drowned. Then I put it in a black plastic sack and left it in the porch for Huw to collect with the rubbish. I thought about getting rid of the hens after that – they are surprisingly dirty creatures – but Huw gave me a mongrel, a short-legged thing with a strong jaw, a good ratter he said. And so far he is right, no more dead hens.

I bought a gooseberry bush the next time I went to town. I found it in the middle aisle of the supermarket, just a thorny stick in a cardboard tube. It won't bear any fruit for a year or two, but when it does, I'm going to make jam. At the sink, when I am washing the dishes, I can see its green leaves through the window.

Train

Outside the pub, the day has shifted again, grey and light-less. It is no longer raining, but the footpaths are wet and a mother passes by pushing a buggy with the plastic rain cover still on. Mismatched buildings line both sides of the street. They seem to be sloping inwards, creating a wind tunnel. In both directions, the street looks the same. Which way? Left or right? I tell myself to sober up, retrace my steps to the shopping centre, collect the car, drive home.

I feel at a loss with no car.

The town is strange and oddly familiar; the streets, the shops, the sky, all the colour of gypsum. I walk on, taking random turns, until I find myself standing outside smart-looking premises.

SEAHORSE ART GALLERY

The exterior is painted coral and stands out from an otherwise drab row of dentist clinics and law firms, with the odd terraced house still in residential use. In the window, the art works on display are mostly well-framed oil paintings and acrylics, and a triptych of wire sculptures in the shape of trees. All are technically impressive, but they lack the clear intention of a real artist.

At college, my work in the graduate show was singled out for praise. Outsized clothes pegs made from graphite holding miniature men's shirts. But when I tried sculpture again in the art collective, I no longer knew what I was doing. The only one who noticed I was struggling was a woman named Julia.

She painted small watercolours that initially I had dismissed as stock, but later saw that they carried beauty in the dark tone of the palette, their oblique symbolism.

She told me . . .

—Just keep working . . .
—Forget about producing anything . . .

And one rainy afternoon, over a cup of tea, I confided in her about having an abortion when I was nineteen.

The following year, when the collective held an exhibition, my found-art sculpture *HI-TIDE* was one of the first pieces to sell, despite the silly price tag I'd put on it. When I phoned Tom to tell him, he was delighted.

—I knew you could do it.

By the end of the evening, there were **SOLD** stickers dotted everywhere. Except on Julia's work. I was a bit drunk by then and would have liked to console her, but my friendship with her had ended, badly, months before that night.

Beyond the window of the Seahorse Art Gallery, I detect shadowy movement, and continue along the street. An old man is handing out religious cards. **BE AWARE OF GOD'S TERMS AND CONDITIONS.**

Where it escapes the clouds, the low winter sun is blinding, and I can feel my headache getting stronger, and a mild nausea in my stomach. I stop a teenager and ask where the Shopping Centre is. They point left, throw a skateboard to the pavement, skate away. I take the next left but all I can see is the train station.

Wouldn't it be a better idea, after nearly three pints, to take a train back to Dublin and collect the car tomorrow?

Did I already suspect that I was done with the car? Done too with the woman who drove it, who loved the quiet click of the door shutting on the world, and the elevated seat from which she could look down on everything? Who secretly loved the way men resented her getting out of it, mostly with her dark sunglasses on?

I don't know.

The Victorian station house has fallen into disrepair. Rain is spilling from a broken gutter. The exterior stone is water-stained and crows are gathering on the ridge tiles. The interior is gutted. Along the platform, at regular intervals, there are square wooden planters containing dead geraniums. A timetable has been stuck inside a wooden frame, but the print is too small to read.

Two men are huddled against the station house. The younger has the sleeves of his hoodie pushed up over his elbows and is carrying a plastic bag of beer cans. The older is wearing jeans that pleat above black shoes. He is saying that his head is 'wrecked'. The younger man rattles up some content from his throat and spits it onto the concrete. I turn away and read a framed poster on the wall.

THINGS YOU MIGHT SEE IN THE BUG HOTEL

Ladybugs
Bees
Beetles
Earwigs
Aphid midges
Wasps

Spiders
Hoverflies

The bug hotel is an amalgam of wood, bricks, bark, corrugated cardboard and chicken wire, but I cannot see anything moving inside, not even a spider.

It begins to rain again. Not heavy, but insistent, and despite the sports socks and runners, the cold seeps up into my legs from the concrete platform. I sit on a bench to read the information on the electronic display board.

The next train to Dublin is in two hours.

STAY BEHIND THE LINE

The older man is staring at me now, so I squint harder at the display board, pretend to be studying it.

When did I start to love the neat lines of the middle classes? Their square houses and square gardens. The symmetrical arrangement of furniture in their rectangular rooms. Their obsession with clean, straight trajectories into the future.

Was it at school when I realised that it was easy to pass as middle class so long as I wore the right clothes, spoke the right way, picked up the right knife in a restaurant?

Or at college when I opted for sculpture over drawing to get a better grade?

Or was it when, at a gig one night, I met a man who was *really* middle class and turned towards him the way a plant turns to light?

Looking back, I see myself forcing my life into a straight line. And looking forward, I see myself continuing to do the same. But there is no straight line back or forward, no line at all, just moments in time, like this one now, on this platform, in the silence of the afternoon.

The bench is damp and my body has clamped shut against the wind. I stand up, stamp my feet.

—You goin' for the ferry?

The sound carries towards me, clean up the platform. It comes from the man with the beers. His accent is local. Familiar broad, flat vowels.

—You're going for the ferry, are ye?

It is not too late, I tell myself. I could phone Tom, tell him it is an emergency. He would come straight away. I imagine him standing in front of me, staring at my short hair and trench coat, bewildered.

The man with the beers is now shuffling towards me, his voice getting louder, his questioning more insistent.

—I said is ye goin' for the ferry?

I hear myself saying *Yes*.

—'Tis on the other platform. Over there. The train'll be along in a few minutes.
—Thank you.
—You'll need a ticket to get on.
—Yes ... Thank you.

I hurry to the ticket machine, press buttons, tap my card. A crackling noise seems to go on forever. And then a ticket drops out.

Crossing the metal bridge to the far platform I bash my shin against the edge of a step.

The past is sliding away from me.

The older man is now standing on the edge of the opposite platform, drinking one of the cans of beer, still staring across at me. There is no sign of the younger one. I stare back, but I am no longer registering him as real. He is just part of a tableau I already know I will remember. The water-stained stone. The dead geraniums. The arc of the tracks disappearing in both directions.

My phone pings. A WhatsApp message from my daughter.

—*no soya milk.*

There are flashing red lights and the glissando-like sound of a train approaching in the distance.

When it stops, passengers alight.

I get up off the bench, walk across the platform, and board the train.

MIND THE GAP

The train pulls out, past housing estates and hedges, then acres of Christmas trees. Fields raked with the last light of the day. Mud. Bungalows with mirrors dangling from fascia boards to prevent swallows nesting. Abandoned factories. Low-lying super barns. Concrete yards. Sheep. Cattle. Yellow and russet ferns. An old church. And running parallel to the train tracks for a mile or more, a brown, slow-moving river.

The frame is blue and green and grey, lead white and charcoal black; the medium is gouache paint, a little faded, watery, all caught in a fine mist. But one line – a distorted horizon – is hard, angular, unforgiving. I catch myself. It has been a long time since I looked at the world as an unpainted painting. I used to do it all the time. When did I forget to remember to look at the world like this?

I sink back into the headrest, leaving my trench coat on. There is a stale taste in my mouth.

A female voice on a phone nearby:

—Sorry now, but I'm going to hang up if you speak to me like that ...
Then the puncture of a pre-recorded announcement.

—LADIES AND GENTLEMEN. IARNRÓD ÉIRE-ANN WELCOMES YOU ON BOARD ...

I ruined my friendship with Julia by having an affair with her son.

She first mentioned him to me at the collective.

Peter was studying for a doctorate, she told me. In neuro-something-physics. He was twenty-nine and still living at home.

I met him a few weeks later when he came to collect an easel for Julia. He was shy and awkward, less than average height with a stocky build, but with nice eyes behind glasses. I doubt if we exchanged three or four sentences, but I took his mobile number in case Julia needed anything. When he left, I noticed him crouching in the yard outside the studio to pet a mangy dog that was lying in the sun.

On the joint pretext of my interest in physics and his in sculpture, we started messaging each other, met for coffee twice, went for a walk once. But it was me who suggested calling to his home when I knew that Julia would be in the studio. Where they lived was a run-down area. I was surprised. I had always presumed that Julia, with her English accent and her manners, was well-to-do. My car at the time was an MPV with a CHILDREN ON BOARD sticker and I felt nervous leaving it parked on the road.

I could say that I was sexually attracted to Peter, or intrigued by him, but it is closer to the truth to say that I was looking for distraction. Desperately looking for distraction. I hadn't yet admitted to myself that I was not an artist, but the knowledge was already beginning to coagulate inside me, bubbling up in panic dreams and days of grey inertia. We had sex on his single bed in a box room full of old books. I reached orgasm quickly but he took longer.

I felt depressed driving home and decided to end it. But a week or so later, I messaged Peter again.

We met in hotel rooms after that, usually at times when

I was meant to be in the studio. Anonymous hotels, near the airport, easy to reach on public transport with plenty of parking. I paid with cash.

I liked Peter. The sex was nice and the conversation could be interesting. But there was no cumulative effect. In my memory, I slept with him only once.

The last time I saw him was in a hotel.

He had wanted us to spend a night together and I had agreed. But the organisation of pickups from school, of meals, of lifts to school the next day, had been exhausting, and by the time I arrived in the hotel room I was tetchy. And unprepared for the sight of Peter. He arrived wearing a shirt still creased from the packet, and holding supermarket flowers. And a box of Belgian chocolates.

I panicked, withdrew to the bathroom with my phone, emerged minutes later saying that my son had hurt his knee playing rugby, and left.

I never saw Peter again.

There were texts, late-night voicemails, a long email in which he said I had been using him. And then nothing.

There was a period of regret afterwards. But it is not true that suffering teaches us anything. In nursing homes, old people who are wise and kind are the rare exceptions. Most are petty and narcissistic. Like the rest of us.

But what I could not have known was that when I turned the key to re-enter my old life, the door would be locked from inside. There was no way back to the relatively content life I'd been living before the affair. Was it only seven years ago?

I thought I could have sex with a man, undress him, kiss him, rub my hands on his chest, take him in my mouth, pull him inside me, cry out with pleasure, and then go home and lie in bed next to my husband and everything would be the same. But it wasn't. Something seeped into our home, our marriage, our bed – a vague doubt, a sense of distance, a loss of laughter, a new secrecy about my body – until one night we were having sex and all I felt was a tremendous sadness. But after a while that faded and I felt nothing much at all.

I drank more after that and had extra-marital sex with three other men:

> A Married Colleague, six times.
> A Young Guy in New York that Elaine never knew about, twice.
> And once with my neighbour Susan's husband, on the couch in the family room, when she was away with children visiting her parents.

I expected Tom to notice that something was wrong, but he never did.

The toilet has been occupied since I boarded the train. When a woman emerges, I hurry down the aisle and enter. It is surprisingly clean and I evacuate easily after the Guinness. The flush is powered by a suction system that leaves the metal bowl spotless. I wash my hands in the compact sink-cum-dryer, flush again, wait for the smell to dissipate before returning to my seat.

Beads of rain streak the window beyond which there is a violet tint in the sky as dusk begins to fall. Dim telegraph poles slip by. Then a chequerboard of yellow and black at the edge of a small town, and bubbled letters caught in the floodlights of an AstroTurf pitch.

RIP DAMO LEGEND

At the next station, faces on the platform smoke cigarettes in a fabular scene. There is the noise of altercation but I cannot see anything. Male abrasive voices. Then a shout. Then nothing. The night absorbs it all.

The train shunts forward, gradually picks up speed, then thrums gently along again. Very few passengers are left on board. Down the aisle, two schoolboys show each other screens and laugh. And further on, the Christmas jingle of a ringtone. A male voice answers the call and speaks in a low, monotonous tone. Over my head lights flicker on and in the black glass, a middle-aged woman with short hair stares back at me.

Outside, the beam of a lighthouse turns in the sky.

The girl with the trolley appears. She is friendly to everyone, even to the man behind me who asks her if she knows what *muckaroo* means.

—Muckaroo!

He tells her it means 'to be in the muck'. Not a 'good thing'. He warns her that she 'wouldn't like it'.

She smiles, tells him she is sure he is right.

I order tea. The girl drops a teabag into a polystyrene cup, pours in hot water. I watch the teabag swimming expertly on the surface.

—Milk?
—Yes.

She passes me the tea, two plastic cartons of UHT milk, three napkins, a wooden stirrer and two sachets of sugar.

The female voice on the phone again:

—Can you hear me now? I said I am sorry for hanging up. But you really shouldn't speak to me like that ...

At the next station, a family with an Eastern European accent get on. The large, pretty mother sits with her two children, a boy and a girl, in the seats in front of me. The father, wearing a brown leather jacket, stands in the gangway connection, shouting orders at the children in English.

—Sit down!
—Keep your jacket on!
—Take your neck scarf off!

The family stirs up memories that I don't want to have, and I am glad when they get off the train again.

When our children were very young, Tom had to travel to make business contacts, *to put his face around*. Once, when he was in Cork for a conference, I got the bright idea of taking the children on the train to join him, of staying the night, and driving back the next day in Tom's car.

—Great idea, he approved.

Tom left mid-week and on Friday morning I took the children to the station with a huge bag of colouring books and crayons, storybooks, lunchboxes, bottles of water. They were well behaved but the train was crowded and not very clean and, as the journey went on, they got tired, I got tired. There were no mobile phones or tablets to distract anyone from boredom.

At one of the stations, a slightly drunk man sat in the narrow seat beside my daughter. He had a naggin of whiskey in a brown paper bag and kept asking her over and over if she was a good girl for her 'Mammy'. I smiled to appease him and smiled to reassure her. He fell asleep as we neared Cork and my mood lifted.

I wiped the children's faces and buttoned their jackets. I freshened my lipstick.

But when we disembarked, Tom was not there. We waited. The platform emptied. I sat on a bench, with a child on either side of me. We waited. The wind shuffled up at intervals, making my eyes water. We waited. The children became cranky. When my son began to whinge, I pulled him onto my lap and scolded my daughter for teasing him. We waited.

Finally, Tom sauntered into view, glowing from a long, luxurious power shower and a full Irish breakfast.

—Where's my little man?
—Where's my princess?
And a guarded kiss for me.
I kissed him back.

My phone pings. A text. From Tom.

—*You home yet?*

I feel immobile, as though everything has already happened. My ankles are cold but my shin is no longer sore and my headache is gone. The lack of shock is shocking.

Nothing is inside me now, only the rhythm of the train. Systole, diastole, systole, diastole.

I text back.

—*Won't be home this evening. Nothing to worry about. Back in touch soon. x*

I wait for the phone to ring. But it doesn't ring.

My finger finds the volume button and clicks it downwards.

Silent Mode On.

There is one image that I return to over and over.

It is of a woman stepping onto a train. It is the same woman as earlier, but her hair is shorter, her clothes are slightly raff-ish, her breath is boozy if you get close. I have slowed the clip down, sped it up, blurred the background, tried deep focus, but there is something in the frame that always eludes me. Why does she step onto the train? It would be so much easier for her to go back to the comfortable house in the suburbs, open a bottle of wine, pet the cat, throw a few crackers and cheese on a plate and nibble at them while watching TV, phone her best friend, smile at her daughter, ask her son how school is going, sink into a hot bath, lie close to her husband in bed at night, letting the heat of his body warm her frozen soul.

This image – of the woman stepping off the platform and onto the train – has come to seem like a demarcation, a before-and-after moment, like my father's death.

But this is just the processing system in my head.

At night in the cottage when I am writing in my notebook, I never know which tense to use, the past or the present. It is the past I am *remembering*, but memory is with me in the present, in every waking hour and even in my dreams, it flashes up in full technicolour – whether I want it or not – on the screen of my mind. And with each recall, memory is altered. When I am content, the memories of life in the house in the suburbs come and go like gentle ghosts, but on days when my mood is low, they haunt me. There is no such thing as a memory, just images whose shape and form are coloured by the present.

I don't think it's like this for everyone.

Sometimes I envy my friend here, Lena. Whenever she talks about *her* past, her account is always the same. And always straightforward. Her father ('the bastard') was a Turkish-Cypriot and her mother ('the idiot') was from Aberdeen and her childhood ('tough') ended early and she became a sex worker ('good money') in Bristol before moving to Wales ('retiring').

The first time I encountered Lena was in April this year. I was lingering over a coffee in the town café when she stopped at my table.

—Hey babes, she addressed me. You all right there? You look a bit lost.

When I didn't reply, she admired the skirt I was wearing. It was one I had bought in a charity shop a few weeks earlier. She said she wanted to paint her kitchen the same colour.

—It's tangerine, I said.
She looked at me intently.
—You all right, though?
—Yes, I told her. Thank you.

I saw her a few weeks later again in the supermarket. I was perusing tomato plants in the middle aisle, considering whether to buy one or not, when she sneaked up on me – she had a talent for this, as I discovered – and whispered in my ear.

—What are you doing for the rest of the day?

My first reaction was irritation at being accosted. But then I couldn't think of anything better to say than the truth.

—Finish shopping . . . get the bus—
—Great! she exclaimed. Glass of wine. My place. I'll drop you home later.

And it was over that first glass of wine that Lena told me about having been a sex worker in Bristol ('Arab men on business trips are the best clients') before moving to Wales with the money she had saved.

She had bought a small site a few miles outside the town and assembled a timber-framed house ('off the internet') on it. The neighbours ('arseholes') had lodged a planning permission complaint against her but lost. Some loophole about a mobile home being on the site.

—Are you not worried about retaliation? I asked her.
—Let the fuckers come.

Whenever she was tipsy, she showed me an old shotgun she kept in a wooden box by the door.

But she asked me nothing about myself.

Ferry

A girl who used to babysit for us – a plain, unremarkable girl – is in the kitchen of our house in the suburbs. But it is not our house in the suburbs, and it is full of children. A baby crawls along a shelf. As it's about to fall . . .

LAST STOP!

The voice wakes me, and for a moment I am unsure of who I am or where I am.

LAST STOP!

The train is stationary and I look through the window. A figure strides past. A platform sign comes into focus. **ROSSLARE EUROPORT**.

Unable to disperse the sense of fear from the dream, I pull my lips together, straighten up and trundle down the aisle. I feel blurred at the edges.

On the platform, it is cold and raining and one of my laces has come undone. When I stoop to tie it, the ends of my trench coat drag on the wet concrete. The opposite platform, where the train runs back towards Dublin, is completely empty.

Except for the schoolboys, who climb into the back of a waiting car, everyone follows a path on which **TERMINUS** is stencilled in yellow paint. I tag on and follow the path too. There is only one goal now, to get inside somewhere warm and dry. The path is so narrow that we have to walk in single file. In front of me, a young man in a red baseball cap moves half a beat slower than I do, so I drop back to avoid catching him. Then he stalls to light a cigarette and I half-run to get ahead of him.

The path widens into a car park with more yellow **TERMINUS** signs. In the beams of passing headlights the rain is silver and the judder of wheels on tarmac give the scene a lurid quality. Beyond artificial lighting, everything is black. I pass two, three more passengers. Despite the cold and the rain, they walk without hurrying, one pulling a plastic wheelie case behind them.

The terminus building is nondescript, but my body revives as it passes through the automatic door. How quickly everything reduces to the need for food, drink, toilet and a place that is safe and warm. Deprived of these, there are only preoccupations.

Inside the terminus it is bright and quiet, like a hospital. There is a string of desks with no one at them, racks of brochures, a roped barrier.

An electronic sign.

CONNECTING EUROPE FOR A
SUSTAINABLE FUTURE

Beside it a poster.

ARE YOU READY FOR BREXIT?

There is a wall-mounted TV, black, its remote control long lost. A leftover from a time before everyone held their own screen in their own hands.

In the toilets I dry my hair under an old-fashioned hand-dryer. I am sweating inside the trench coat. The woman in the mirror is pale now and her eyes are red-rimmed. But I do not struggle to recognise her. She is me.

The girl at the hatch of the Coffee Dock has a friendly smile.

—Is it still raining out there?

I nod, order a mint tea to settle my stomach, and a bottle of water.

I pick a clean table to sit at. The table beside me is covered in empty coke bottles, a rolled-up newspaper and a lighter that must be broken.

The girl with the friendly smile comes out of a side door and sweeps the rubbish into a plastic bag, sprays the table with a cleaning product, wipes it down.

I forget to add water to the tea and it scalds my mouth, leaving my tongue feeling smooth as a descaled fish. I take a swig of the water.

WHEN OPENING HOLD CAP FIRMLY AND POINT AWAY FROM PEOPLE AND FRAGILE OBJECTS

Bored, I empty out the contents of my handbag onto the table.

Wallet
Phone
Packet of tissues
Hand cream
USB flash drive
Protein bar
Sunglasses
Lipstick
A powder compact
A folding hairbrush

Receipts
Two safety pins
One hooped earring
An eyeliner
Three pens
An assortment of coins
A shopping trolley token
A travel-size perfume

More foot passengers arrive in the terminus. A grungy girl with a colourful skirt and wool socks scrunched down above hiking boots. Judging from her accent I think she is French, but I overhear her telling the Coffee Dock girl that she is from Luxembourg. She strikes up a conversation with an older Irish man who is wearing a hat. She wants to know where she can buy tobacco. I am amazed at her ease, how she manages to be friendly but not sexual, to give off just the right vibe.

—Nice to meet you. No, Luxembourg. Yes, a lot of people think that . . .

I watch her stow her rucksack in a locker afterwards and then head out of the terminus, presumably to follow the instructions the man has given her about where to buy tobacco.

—Go on up the hill there till you get to the petrol station and if it's not open go on further up the hill there on to the hotel there and if that's . . .

I imagine the blackness of the night outside, the lonely desolation of ports, the coldness of the rain, and her giving a cheery hello to everyone she meets.

A stocky man in a tracksuit walks by with a pug in a harness. The pug's tail is curled upwards revealing a bright pink anus. The young man in the red baseball cap checks the soles of his runners for dirt. A man with two young children – a chatty girl of about six and a quiet boy of about three – is at the Coffee Dock. He is gentle with them, but the girl's hair has not been brushed for a few days and the boy sucks a soother. I wonder where their mother is. Perhaps she has disappeared. When a woman disappears, the chances are that she has been murdered by someone she knows, most likely her husband or her boyfriend or someone she has been having sex with.

But women can disappear right in front of you.

My mother began disappearing in her fifties, and by seventy, she was completely gone. Sometimes, when I was visiting her in the nursing home, I had to close my eyes to recover the mother I had known.

My best friend, also. After marriage and children, she disappeared into a story called My Perfect New Life.

My daughter. Not a mother yet, but already on her way to disappearing into the role of Perfect Young Woman. Exactly the role I brought her up to play.

The father with the two young children buys drinks and snacks from the Coffee Dock and takes them to a table out of view. The girl with the friendly smile is trying to look busy, even though there is no work to do. She wipes the countertop, cleans the coffee machine, wipes the countertop again. She has the local radio station on, and I catch bits of pop songs from the noughties.

—boy . . . for a day . . . what I wanted . . .

Two men in hi-vis jackets appear, one carrying a clipboard, the other doing the talking. They start with the older Irish man, asking questions, ticking boxes with a pen.

I have a feeling that there is something to dread, but also that there's been a break in the circuit and I've forgotten what it is that I am dreading.

On my phone there are three missed calls from Tom, a voicemail, one text message, and four WhatsApp messages.

I text back.

—I am going away for a short while but please don't worry, I'll be back soon. Tell the kids I am visiting a friend. x

I walk across to the Customer Service Desk, dumping my handbag and most of its contents into a bin on the way, and press the bell. An assistant, still wearing the half-smile of a shared joke, comes out from the back. She is dressed in a navy fleece top with company logo and navy slacks and is friendly in a business-like way, tapping the keyboard, asking questions by rote.

—What is your destination tonight?
—Any bags to check in?
—Card or cash?
—One way or return?

As her questions gather pace and I respond to each, my voice sounds like it is coming from far away, like the sea inside a shell.

By the time the pair in hi-vis jackets reach me, I am ready.

—Foot passenger?
—Yes.
—Can I see your boarding pass? Thank you. Any bags?
—No.

I wish I'd had a row with Tom at the train station in Cork, instead of always pretending in front of the children that everything was fine. I wish I had told him that he was a *selfish prick*. Then he could have shouted back that his *fucking work was fucking tiring*. Maybe then we could have laughed or hugged or decided to divorce. Anything would have been better than turning ourselves into bit actors in a play called *The Perfect Family*.

Or maybe I am wrong? I don't know. But at the very least I should have said something to him afterwards, when we were alone. I should have told him how I felt while waiting on that platform. But it is easier to pretend than to be real.

My phone pings. A WhatsApp message from Mark.

—*can I get a lift.*

He must be out of after-school study by now.

I see him arriving home, ravenous, the house empty except for Lauren on her laptop in the attic, a cereal bowl on the floor beside her.

My left hand tightens around the phone while the fingers on my right mechanically press apps and widgets.

I reply.

—*held up at work x*

I depress the side button and the screen turns black. Some analgesic force has taken over and I am just drifting along now.

Another man in a hi-vis jacket appears.

ALL FOOT PASSENGERS TO BOARD
THE SHUTTLE BUS

There is an expanse of tarmac to be crossed in order to reach the bus. In the darkness it looks like a river. The air is windless and smells different to how it does during the day: sharper and full of mortality.

On the bus, the door remains open, letting in cold.

Slowly, in ones and twos, people emerge from the terminus, like particles thrown into the night. Some are familiar: the grungy girl; the older Irish man, but now without his hat; the man without his pug now. Some are not: a family of tourists; a lone guy with headphones. Where had they been? Was there some other part of the terminus I was unaware of?

There are free double seats, but a woman with an apologetic smile stops beside mine. She tries to stow her bag in the overhead rack, but she cannot reach that high, and a queue backs up behind her. The man without his pug stands up to help her and she collapses in beside me, her cheap perfume colonising the surrounding air. I move closer to the window, irritated that she has chosen me. How safe I must look.

Eventually the doors close, the lights dim, and we dip out into the night. Behind me the propulsive sound of a chase leaks out into the night. The lone guy with the headphones is playing a game on his phone.

My organs are marbled with coldness.

The woman with the apologetic smile holds her mouth in a curve, but her eyes dart about, and then, when she is satisfied the coast is clear, she starts to talk. First, the weather. And then she tells me that she is going to the funeral of her brother.

—I am sorry to hear that, I tell her.

She has thin hair fluffed into a halo shape through which her scalp is visible. As she speaks, her lipstick slips into thin tributaries that trickle from her mouth. A smoker's giveaway. Her accent is hybrid, a lost rural Ireland and a provincial urban England. It stretches and contracts in unexpected places, forcing me to concentrate in order to hear perfectly familiar words.

—He'd been ill for a long time but it's a shock all the same when it happens . . .

I take out my phone, turn it on. I do not want to engage in conversation with this woman.

Four more missed calls, five text messages and eleven WhatsApp messages, including one from my best friend. I hesitate. Then I open the message from Elaine.

—*Hey there! We would love to see you guys at our place Saturday before the Holidays anytime after 3* 🌞 🌲 🎁

She has not been contacted yet.

There is something ridiculous about a grown woman referring to another woman as her best friend, but this is how I have always thought of Elaine.

The last time we met was in a Korean restaurant in the city that she had suggested. It had taken her ages to arrange, what with her work schedule, and her husband's work schedule, and the au pair being UNBELIEVABLY AWKWARD, but I was looking forward to seeing her.

I remember the half glass of beer that she sipped; the 'bibi-something' with seafood that she picked at; how shiny her cheekbones were, as though they'd been coated in clingfilm; how the screen of her phone kept flashing on the table beside us while we were talking.

She took the phone with her when she went to the bathroom in the middle of the meal, and she returned in a hurry.

—I have to get back, she explained. Sorry. The little one is playing up. We'll do it again. Soon.

I had ordered a glass of red wine and the house 'special', which turned out to be rice with vegetables, a lot of chilli, soy sauce, sliced beef and a fried egg. I was enjoying the food and had already finished the wine. The conversation thus far had been standard – a speech from her about the treatment of mothers in the workplace, attempts from me to make Skype calls with my brother sound funny – but I'd expected, as the night wore on, that we would get to the 'real' stuff. Whatever that might have been.

I stayed on in the restaurant after she left, ordered another glass of wine and accepted the complimentary shot of sake. A work group at the nearby table grew lively and one of the party, a middle-manager type, bumped the back of my chair on the way back from the Gents.

My plan had been to get a taxi home and pick up the car the next morning, but I joined the lively work group, let the middle-manager press his thigh against mine and tell me how he was going to retire early and move to Vietnam, open a hostel over there, get out of the rat race . . .

I drank a great deal more wine and another shot of sake, and I drove home instead of getting a taxi, way over the limit.

Elaine had been my best friend in school, and despite our different paths – teaching, marriage and children for me; a career in marketing and single-girl fun for her – we had remained 'best friends'. Until she hit thirty-nine, met a guy in a bar one night, and married him within a year. A guy so anodyne that I had to remind myself to include him in conversation. Canadian. Younger than her. Did something in technology. Handsome in a Ken Doll sort of way.

Then the kids – 'babygirl' first, and a year later, 'the little one' – and suddenly the BRAND NEW LIFE brand had begun and I had to learn to pick up on its cues:

No Stories of Past Escapades in front of Perfect Husband.
And later.
No Stories of Past Escapades at all.

I tried to be happy for Elaine. I organised her pre-wedding party at a Spa Resort Hotel. I was person-of-honour at her humanist wedding. I was guide parent to babygirl, special auntie to the little one. But I was not happy for her, I was heartbroken.

I kept telling myself that we would find our groove again. But we never did.

Beside me, the woman with the apologetic smile shifts again in her seat, preparing to give me another try. But I refuse to look up from the phone. I hear her thinking

—*Here I am, travelling to the funeral of my brother, and she couldn't care less. What a cow!*

And she is right.

She roots around pointedly in her handbag and takes out a packet of hard toffees. She opens them, pops one in her mouth, and offers one to me. I decline. The final blow. We will not speak again. I hear the sweet rattling around in her mouth, its sweetness fuelling her thoughts. She has picked a dud, she thinks, but not to worry, and then, ever the pragmatist, she glances around for a better candidate.

Part of me would like to tap her on the shoulder and tell her that I am on a road trip because I could not stand to put one more plate into the dishwasher. Or load the washing machine one more time. Or remember to buy cat food. Or pick hoodies off the couch. Or put shoes away in wardrobes. Or pair socks. Or change bedsheets. Or take out rubbish. Or ask my son to tidy his bedroom. Or chop carrots. Or run bleach around the inside of a toilet bowl. Or think about presents people might like for birthdays. Or make a list of who to send cards to at Christmas. Or have predictable sex with my husband. Or go to dinner parties. Or plan summer holidays. Or shop around online for car insurance. Or stay on hold, listening to Vivaldi, while trying to cancel a subscription for a magazine. Or check labels on ice cream to make sure there is no gelatine so my daughter can eat it. Or watch another box set on Netflix. Or make my mouth form words to have the same conversations about work-life balance. Or wipe toothpaste spits off the sink in the bathroom. Or plan to go to the gym and not go. Or wash one more yogurt carton to put in the recycling bin . . .

But it is not true that I am on a road trip because of any of that. I am not even on a road trip, I'm on a ferry at night crossing the Irish Sea. And what *is* true is that I don't know why.

I am not angry with the woman with the apologetic smile.

I am angry with Elaine.

In the Korean restaurant what I wanted to say to Elaine, as she gathered up her pashmina, threw €50 on the table and kissed me on both cheeks, was that while it is *nice* to have children – I have children myself – you have not created a super race of humans who will save the world – you have simply put more people on an overcrowded planet.

She had been sorry for me over our meal. I saw it in her eyes. Sorry for me that I was jaded and behind the times. Sorry that I drank too much. Sorry that my husband and children were not *everything* to me.

She told me she wanted to be 'clean'.
I heard 'chosen,' 'saved,' 'baptised'.
The same old story I have heard a thousand times. *Humans Remaking the World as Paradise.*

I was tired of friendship with women. With mothers at the school gates. With neighbours. With work colleagues. With my best friend. I tired of coffee dates, lunch dates, WhatsApp group chats, text messages, phone calls, spa breaks, city breaks, 'Girls' nights out', 'Girls' nights in'.

It was exhausting, like playing whack-a-mole. I had only just finished with one friend when another was due attention, and someone or other was always slightly peeved at being short-changed in this never-ending game.

But the alternative to this was isolation. No in-between. We were each other's consolation prizes, but also each other's police. With the restraint of silence and of disapproval, Mothers prevent each other from straying too far.

Friendships between women exist. But with fine print.

My bloodstream is full of cortisol again.

At the mouth of the ferry, the bus comes to a halt and sits there trembling in the darkness.

A huge crane is draped in Christmas lights and stands out against the sky like an earthbound constellation. Below it, stacks and stacks of corrugated containers in blue and orange and brown.

Trucks loop around the tarmac in a heavy yet graceful choreography, wending their way inside the ferry. Truck after truck after truck, packed in like matches in a matchbox, to be transported across the sea to warehouse, factory, supermarket depot. Full of potatoes and designer furniture, canned goods and Vietnamese stowaways, plastic tubs of sweets.

Conversations cease as we come to a halt at the entrance to the ferry. Even the video game falls silent. We are all on pause now, waiting to sail out over the Irish Sea on a cold November night. With the heating on, the air in the bus smells of reheated soup. And then, suddenly, the engine cuts and we are inside the hold. I stay seated while the woman with the apologetic smile stands up, arranges her scarf, waits for the first gap to appear and then pounces into the aisle.

I am last to get off.

The interior of the ferry looks like a hotel, with brushed steel wall lamps and patterned carpet and signs for bars and restaurants, and even a gold card lounge.

I need a drink.

The **COSMOPOLITAN BAR** is an over-lit realm of faux leather couches and chenille upholstered chairs. It is almost empty but there is a permanent low rumble and a safety announcement on repeat.

—*Emergency Help Points . . . Lifejackets . . . CCTV . . . Emergency Help Points . . .*

There is a small queue at the self-service counter. In front of me, a boy of about twelve and a young couple in identical puffer jackets. The couple are taking a long time to select their food.

—Is there egg in that?
—Could we get a main without the meal deal?
—We don't actually want desserts.

The boy cuts in front of them and pays for a single can of cola with exact change.

On my tray is a single screw-top half bottle of red wine. When I get bored waiting, I put another on the tray, along with a 'garden' salad under a hard plastic dome.

The girl behind the counter has brown hair in a tight ponytail and a Welsh accent.

—Very quiet this evening, she tells me. Less than a hundred, I'd say.

—What about the lorry drivers? I ask.

—Oh, we never see them. They have their own lounge. Are you from Dublin?

—No, I . . .

—Your accent. It sounds like . . .

—I'm from a seaside town.

She scans the two bottles of wine and places a glass on my tray.

—Might be a bit rough tonight.

—Yes.

At a table battened to the carpet with metal screws, I take off my trench coat, twist the cap on one of the bottles and pour to the top of the glass. The wine floods my mouth, releasing a wave of tannin-fuelled acedia. Another mouthful and space rolls away between me and the house I left this morning. Beyond the bubbled windows the sea is not visible, but I know it is out there, moving incessantly in the darkness, and as the ferry drifts further from shore, I have an intense sensation of the entropy of all things.

I take the hard plastic dome off the salad. Lettuce, ham, slices of tomato. I eat a bit. And then cover it up again, quickly.

On my phone, there's an SMS informing me that I am on a different network and that calls and texts are charged at international rates. Also, six more WhatsApp messages, two more missed calls, and another email from work. I don't read any of them. Instead I compose an email resigning from my teaching position with immediate effect.

While I am re-reading it, I wonder if it is possible that two typed sentences can change a life?

But before the neurons in my brain can generate any more electrical signals which lead to thought, I press Send.

I type HOTELS FISHGUARD into Google, tap the first search result, press the PHONE symbol.

   —PLEASE HOLD WHILE WE TRY TO CONNECT YOU

Then a real voice.

   —Hello?
   —Can I book a room for tonight? Single. Yes. On the ferry. Yes. See you then.

After one half bottle of wine, my body is at home in its new environment, including the din from a nearby rotating fan.

A sign on a fire door reads like a joke written especially for me.

PUSH BAR TO OPEN

The woman with the apologetic smile pauses at the entrance to the Cosmopolitan Bar. She glances in, sees me, waves, and continues on her way. I don't wave back, but I am impressed by how quickly she has reset herself to forgiveness mode.

I twist the cap on the second half bottle of red wine. There is the clicking sound of a seal breaking. But the effect is more predictable now. A wave strong enough to maintain unreality, but only so long as I keep drinking.

I usually get sentimental on red wine. Manufactured emotion, even if it is sadness, is always pleasing.

But I am not sentimental tonight.

It was a charge that Julia had levelled at my work.

I had shown her a textile piece that I had been working on, a huge heart made from scraps of old clothing belonging to Lauren and Mark entitled *IMPRINT*.

Everyone else had loved it. But Julia deemed it 'sentimental'.

She was the only truly honest person I knew at that time, though she never mentioned my affair with her son.

There is still an inch of wine in the second bottle, so I spread my trench coat over the back of the chair when I need to leave the table.

In the toilets some of the bowls are unflushed and one has dried blood on the seat. With the movement of the ship, the white tiles under my feet appear to be undulating as I wash my hands. There is a burst of noise and a group of teenage girls enter. I watch them in the mirror. They laugh loudly while one of them swipes right on her phone. They speak Spanish, but they look like teenage girls everywhere: hoodies and trainers, leggings that showcase their vulvas.

In the duty-free shop I pick up a half bottle of vodka, a phone charger and a travel toothbrush set.

My table has been cleared when I get back to the lounge. I consider getting another bottle of wine, but the ferry is swaying more now and I don't want to risk being sick.

KEEP YOUR BELONGINGS ON YOUR PERSON

I take my trench coat and sit closer to a giant TV screen to distract myself from the swaying. A football match is on and a few tables away, an athletic young man in luxury sportswear smiles at me, thinking I am interested in the game. When he gets up to go to the bar at half-time, he offers to buy me a drink. I decline, smile on autopilot.

—He should've pulled that one back there.
His accent is Welsh.
I smile again.

In a parallel universe, my husband is at home, sitting on the couch, making the exact same comment to our son.

—He should've pulled that one back there.

But tonight, that is not what he is doing.

I feel something clench in my chest, then a ripple of nausea. There is a moment of horror when I think I might throw up, but it passes.

By now, Tom will have phoned around.

I picture him on the couch, being comforted by Susan, who will have testified at this stage to my strange behaviour that morning. WhatsApp messages are firing back and forth. Friends are 'shocked', 'saddened', 'there for him', 'offering to bring over a hot meal'. But mostly thrilled. A pebble has been thrown on the surface of boredom.

In the attic, with the cat beside her on the bed, my daughter is on her phone, emoting.

There is real emotion in there somewhere, but it is so layered in synthetic emotion that it is not possible for her to detach one from the other. Allowing no time-lapse between feeling something uncomfortable and expelling the uncomfortable feeling with instant communication is a brilliant 'trick'. And once discovered, it is impossible to resist. Also, the pull to be the centre of attention is always just that bit more powerful than the pull of genuine feeling.

I wish I hadn't told her so often to cheer up, to smile, to be happy.

But what difference would it have made – saying things – when she spent her teenage years watching me anaesthetise myself with wine every night of the week. No wonder her drug of choice is Xanax.

My son, irritated by the disturbance, is in his room, eating pizza out of a box, trying to study for an upcoming Geography exam.

Afterwards, he will smoke weed out the window, go to bed, sleep. His first reaction to everything ... *how does this affect me?*

I asked him once, when he was in an agreeable mood, what kind of girls – or boys – he liked.

—Girls, he said.
—What kind?

I was expecting tall, short, blonde, brunette ...

—ND, he told me.
—ND?
—No Drama.

The athletic young man in luxury sportswear is back and slapping his thigh.

—Here we go!

The second half of the match is kicking off.

After Mark was born, Tom had a vasectomy. I remember he was watching a football match on TV when I suggested it and he agreed immediately.

—Do you not want to take some time to think about it?
—Nah ... we don't want any more children ... you don't want to stay on the pill ... it makes sense.

His eyes had drifted quickly back to the TV screen.

And it did make sense. So why, pouring myself another glass of wine in the kitchen afterwards, had I been so upset? Because what I had wanted from Tom – for once in his whole goddamn life – was an emotional reaction rather than logic.

But what Tom wanted most was no traffic on the way to work, no conflict at home, no opinions that went too far in any direction. Nothing was worth unsettling his chemical balance for, except maybe the need for cycle lanes in the city. He was passionate about that.

This shortened bandwidth of emotion – where had it come from? That expensive school he went to with its institutional bullying? The same one we sent Mark to?

The mix of sound frequencies from the TV and the engine and the rotating fan creates a somnambulant mood and I shut my eyes. My body is heavy and my brain powers down, swimming in and out of drowsiness in which half-dreams creep and mass together in shadows, dispersing again each time consciousness threatens to surface.

By the time the ferry docks, I am almost asleep.

Have I always known that one day I would make this journey again? Taking 'the boat' across the Irish Sea? I'm not sure. But something tonight feels like the ending of something that started when I was nineteen. Or maybe it ended when my mother died and this is some sort of delayed reaction?

After my father died, when I was eleven, I felt nothing for a long time. I just broke my life into two pieces – happy before his death and less happy after.

This wasn't really accurate, but it was how my brain preferred to arrange things. I did this again when I was nineteen and had an abortion – Before and After – and again when I married Tom, except that then it was Happy Ever After.

When my father died, my mother was the age I am now. Back then, this was old for a woman. As a widow, she was expected to keep house, bring up her children, and go to Mass every Sunday. Nothing else. No wonder she didn't cope with what happened when I was nineteen.

I can still see her face turning from the sink to look at me while I tried to get the words out. The fear that was in her eyes. And then the way she snapped off her pink rubber gloves, pulled a chair out from the table, signalled for me to sit down.

It takes years to remember feelings you make yourself forget.

In September this year, I thought I saw Tom outside the post office in the village.

But it wasn't Tom.

It was a man the same height as him, standing erect like him, wearing a jacket and cords that he might wear, but when the man turned round, he was not Tom.

I felt a sharp flood of disappointment.

This is the thing with feelings. You project and project, but you can never tell how you will feel until an event actually happens.

On the walk home afterwards, I remembered something I had forgotten.

Six, seven years ago I had a mini breakdown.

It was shortly after finishing the affair with Peter. I was cooking Sunday dinner – peeling, chopping, basting, skewering, getting timings wrong, recalculating, trying to keep the meat hot while the vegetables cooked, whipping cream for out-of-season strawberries.

I went out to the hall and called the kids and Tom, telling them that dinner was ready.

My husband appeared first. He had been watching a football match in the den.

—Doesn't this look lovely? he enthused.

Then my son, bleary-eyed from playing computer games.

Finally, my daughter, phone in hand.

I was serving the carrots when it happened.

I put down the dish, moved my plate out of the way, and rested my head on the table. Tom told the children I wasn't feeling well and got me upstairs and into bed. Later that afternoon, a locum doctor came to examine me, a young man with an earnest face. My own GP was a woman my age, inclined to speak quickly into the middle distance, eager to write scripts – sleeping pills, Xanax, Fluoxetine – aware that there is no cure for disappointment. A get-back-on-the-horse kind of woman. This doctor *did* things. Discreetly opened a button. Listened to his stethoscope. Took my pulse. Blood pressure. Temperature. I half-expected leeches next. Behind him, Tom, his head dipped, was already sending out WhatsApp messages, playing his favourite role: the good husband.

I was off work for three weeks with a sick note that said *stress-related illness.* For months afterwards Tom was nervous around me.

And then everything returned to *normal.*

The strategies I adopted over the years to live happily in that house in the suburbs were pretty good. Most of the time they worked. But the problem is a matter of physics. Energy can neither be created nor destroyed, it can only be transferred or changed from one form to another.

It is the same with feelings.

Hotel

A voice comes through the PA system: **ALL FOOT PASSENGERS TO THE RECEPTION AREA.**

I recognise most of the foot passengers by now, but near me there is a husband&wife I haven't noticed before. Him tall and wiry; her stocky with thick glasses. Without any introduction, the wife tells me they were in Ireland buying swans to add to their collection of stone ornaments. The husband remarks that stone ornaments are much cheaper in Ireland.

—We leave our car in the car park—
—And travel by foot—
—It is much cheaper—
—And there is an excellent bus service to Wexford—
—Where we buy the ornaments.

On the carpet at their feet are two lumps wrapped in newspaper.

—They must be heavy, I remark.

The wife explains that the swans are hollow in the middle.

I don't know what else to say and a silence opens up.

—Careful they don't fly off on you! A voice chimes in.

It is the athletic young man in luxury sportswear, now carrying a duffle bag.

The wife throws her head back and bursts into peals of laughter. I laugh too and the athletic young man in luxury sportswear introduces himself.

—Derec with a 'c' instead of a 'k'.

He has a light beard on a featureless face.

I ask the group about local taxis, explaining that I am staying at a nearby hotel.

—Which one? Derec asks.
—Harbour View.
—That's just ten minutes. I'll drop you.

Outside it is no longer raining, but the ground is glassy underfoot.

I follow Derec across the car park. He is not tall, not short, not fat, not thin. He is wearing new-looking runners, track-suit bottoms, grey hoodie under a down jacket.

Without warning, he stops, lights a cigarette, holds it between his middle and ring finger, takes a few quick drags, then flicks it at a bush.

—Wait here. I'll be back in a minute.

And he is gone, zipping between vehicles.

The car park is near empty, bright in some zones, dark in others, yellow markings scored across it: semicircles, circles, squares, rectangles.

My phone is dead. I forgot to plug in the new charger on the ferry.

I calculate that it must be after ten o'clock.

The wind is buffering from all sides now, swirling in gusts that form and unform with anarchic restlessness. I pull up the collar on my trench coat.

A car pulls alongside me. A dark saloon. I think it is Derec. But when the window slides down, I see an older man in a blazer. It is hard to hear him above the wind and he has to shout.

—Are you going to the village?
—Thank you, but I'm waiting for someone.
A pause.
—Suit yourself.

I watch the red tail lights vanish in the darkness.

Maybe I should have taken his offer of a lift.

Derec is taking such a long time coming back.

Maybe I would have been safer with the older man . . .

This second-guessing of potential danger is inescapable for a lone woman at night. But *so* tiring. The endless calculation of risk. And the knowledge that if you get it wrong, it will be 'your own fault'.

At sixteen, Lauren was full of soundbites from TV and the internet.

—My right to walk alone at night.
—My choice to wear a short skirt or bralette.
—My decision to hook up on a dating app.

And she was perfectly justified in her thinking.

But some dangers don't change. They just morph.

It was not 'strangers' in dark saloon cars that my daughter needed to fear when she was sixteen. It was her own friends.

One night she arrived home upset after a party, her make-up blotched, her tights ripped. I told Tom to stay in bed, that I would handle it. And that is exactly what I did. I put on my pink dressing gown, made tea and *handled* the situation.

First, **SANITISE THE LANGUAGE**. If we don't *say* 'assault', then it is *not* assault. It is behaviour, with the suffix *inappropriate* attached.

Second, **DAMAGE LIMITATION**. No reporting to the Guards. *That* would only make things worse. No need for emergency contraception. Boys raised on a diet of porn prefer *mouths* to vaginas.

Third, **NEVER SPEAK ABOUT IT AGAIN**. Organise a 'girls' trip' to the Spa Resort. To cheer things up.

My response was no better than my own mother's had been, all those years ago, when I was nineteen, and came to her upset.

First, she **SANITISED THE LANGUAGE**: If we don't say 'pregnant', then it is not a pregnancy, it is a *problem*, preferably with the suffix *little* attached.

Second, she **LIMITED THE DAMAGE**: the 'boat' to England, the clinic in London, a night in a budget hotel, home again.

Third, she **NEVER SPOKE ABOUT IT AGAIN**: I went back to college the following week, with maternity sanitary towels chaffing the insides of my thighs.

When Lauren was older, I tried to bring up what had happened to her that night. But it was too late. She closed like a snare at the first mention of it. Exactly as I had done when my mother attempted to broach the subject of the abortion with me in the nursing home.

But who am I to tell this story about my daughter?

When I was a child, the body of a newborn baby was found on a beach in Kerry. It had been stabbed to death. A few months before this, a schoolgirl had died giving birth in Longford. And as recently as five or six years ago, a mass grave containing the remains of babies and children was discovered in Tuam.

I was in my twenties when condoms and soft-porn magazines became widely available in Ireland. I still remember the shock of seeing them on shelves in pharmacies and newsagents, the shock I experienced looking at centrefolds, the shock of understanding clearly for the first time how sexual arousal is hardwired for visual stimulation, and that this was not just confined to men.

Not one person at my secondary school was 'openly' gay in the 1980s. And I was almost in my thirties before homosexuality was decriminalised in the state.

But a decade later, when gay marriage and abortion were legalised – SUDDENLY – there was a shiny new story to tell, to ourselves and to the world. That Ireland was now a 'completely different' country. That these were 'more enlightened' times. And that all that bad stuff – sexual abuse, mother and child homes, Magdalene laundries, murdered babies, unbearable shame – was far behind us.

But there are *still* stories that no one wants to tell.

> That we use electronic devices to distract our children because we are too tired to interact with them, too scared to let them roam.
> That we believe the most important thing for our children is that they achieve good grades in examinations,

so they can 'get on' in life.

That our children take drugs at the weekend to relieve
the stresses of the school week and that we don't care
so long as it doesn't interfere with their grades.

That in early teens our children access hardcore pornog-
raphy, violence and extreme ideology on their electronic devices.

That one in three of our older teenagers take anti-
depressants.

When one nightmare disappears, it is easy if there is no *real*
reckoning, for another, just as dark, to slip in to take its place.

A car horn sounds in the distance.

I feel tired. And heavy, as if there is sand in my legs. I have a deep longing to sit down, even on a cold pavement, and wait for whatever is going to happen next.

The night has created an appetency for memories I don't want.

The sky around the moon is black.

Headlights swoop, catching me in their beam, and a lime green coupe pulls up. Derec hops out, puts my plastic bag containing the vodka, the charger and the travel toothbrush set in the boot, while I lower myself into the front passenger seat.

The car is not new and it has mileage on the clock, but it has been modified for speed and is spotless. A dashcam is suctioned to the windscreen and a pair of fluffy dice dangle from the rear-view mirror. The only other disturbance to the interior is his neatly folded jacket on the back seat.

The heating is on, but for a while the car is overpowered by the amount of cold that a metal container can absorb when left all day in a car park in Fishguard in November.

I cannot think of anything to say.

In the silence, I can hear pressure being put on clutch and brake and accelerator, muscles contracting and loosening, fingers moving the gear stick, close to my thigh. I watch Derec's hands on the steering wheel. Square palms. Short fingers. Nails clipped straight. A tattoo on his right wrist. A rose with a date alongside the stem. The car is going faster than I would normally like.

I am surprised by a sensation of lust, the simple heat of it, the blood flowing into my vagina and clitoris. I have no desire for kissing or foreplay, just a desire to fuck or to go down on his cock while he's driving and bring myself off in that position. Yes, it would be easy. And Derec would be perfect. Not attractive. But clean, and uncomplicated. I picture his penis. Smooth and pink with uniformly trimmed pubic hair. I imagine it getting hard in my mouth, moving back and forth against my throat . . .

When I was younger, I would never have looked sexually at a man like this. All my energy was consumed in thinking about how I looked, specifically to older, cerebral types. Men like Derec were invisible to me. Now I marvel at these well-made young guys. Their calves and buttocks, shoulders and arms. The sheer volume of them, in shops and bars and walking the streets. And it is not simply sexual attraction, although there is that as well. It is the sheer availability of them.

I didn't want fun when I was young. I wanted passion, and then, when I found out how painful passion can be, I wanted the certainty of marriage to a man like my husband as a means of protection against passion.

Derec is speaking in his lilting Welsh accent.

—I take the ferry over as much as I can. But, you know, it's not easy, with work and everything. In fact, it's a pain. But about once a month or so. To see my daughter. Yes. She lives with her mother in Kilkenny. Do you know it? A nice town, but not my cup of Bovril. She's six, you know. A smasher.

Really bright and creative. Loves learning things. Getting on great in school. But her mother's a C-U-N-T.

The change in tone is so abrupt that it catches me off guard.

—Sorry?

—I tried going to court. But, you know, that's no use. They always side with the mother, don't they? She took her out of the country when the child was three. I didn't even know where she was for five months or more. Did anyone do anything? Like fuck, they did. If a father did it? You know what I mean. He'd be arrested . . .

—I am sorry to hear that.

His eyes shoot from the road to me, checking that I am not being sarcastic.

I can taste chemicals from an air freshener in my mouth.

—Any kids yourself?

—No.

I expect a follow-up question.

But Derec has no more questions. And neither do I.

I am glad when the road curves upwards and the clustered lights of a village come into view.

You expect it will be a catastrophe that changes how you see the world, not something as mundane as a bottle of champagne being plonked on a marble island, or the sight of your husband caught in the light from a fridge as he searches for cheese.

When Tom arrived home early that night of the cheese and champagne, I already knew that I bored him as much as he bored me. As I heard his keys dropping into the ceramic bowl, I thought: *Is this how it is for everyone?*

When did it happen? When did every crunch of toast, every flushing of a toilet, every radar phone alarm, start to irritate me? When he failed to meet me at the train station in Cork? While we were holidaying in France? Or was it when he said, without ever really looking at any of them, that every piece of sculpture I did was 'brilliant'?

Sometimes I fantasised that Tom was abusive. Nothing terrible. Not coercive control or violence. Just something unpleasant, so that I would have to leave him. A gambling addiction, say, or sexual impropriety in the workplace.

Without justification, it is not easy to end a marriage when there are children involved.

Tom is a good man. He would have agreed to a divorce.

But all that upheaval and damage to the children? For what? Less money and more complication?

So I doubled down on The Happy Marriage story, the same as most people do.

Derec points through the windscreen, interrupting my thoughts.

—There's the Harbour View now.

The hotel is on the crest of the low hill we are climbing, overlooking the village. An assemblage of buildings. Probably an original nineteenth-century house, with various extensions all plastered and painted white and gathered under a HARBOUR VIEW HOTEL sign. A scattering of cars and vans are parked in the car park and under a lean-to roof, near the main entrance, a man is smoking a cigarette. There is another man sitting at a timber picnic bench in the courtyard, but they are not speaking to each other. The man hunched under the lean-to has an Irish look about him.

Derec parks the coupe in front of the hotel's entrance but leaves the engine running.

—Do you fancy a drink? he asks.

He looks at me directly. There is no mistaking his meaning.

I am tempted. But 'C-U-N-T' is still in my ears.

—No.

He reaches under the seat and releases the boot. As soon as I have taken my plastic bag, he floors the accelerator, drives away.

On the steps at the entrance to the hotel, I pause beneath a CCTV camera. The paint on the door is chipped, but the fanlight above is original.

The guy under the lean-to stares at me.

—Hi, I greet him.
He nods back.
—How's it goin'? he asks, in a soft Donegal accent.

The woman at the reception desk starts a smile but doesn't finish it. The roots of her mahogany hair are white.

—Hi. I booked a room. A few hours ago?
I give her my name.
She taps the keyboard and squints at the screen.
—Room 41. Cash or card?

For a second, my brain blanks.

—Card.
—Breakfast is extra.
—Great. Thank you.
—Breakfast is served between seven and nine-thirty.
—Perfect.
—In there.
She gestures towards what looks like a bar, hands me a key card.

The room is up wine-carpeted stairs. It consists of twin single beds with cerise bed runners and cushions, a wardrobe, two lockers with lamps, a unit with a tiny kettle in one drawer, a locked-down hairdryer in the other, a full-length mirror, a wall-mounted TV, a laminated fire plan and three framed prints of fishing boats. Beside the sink, arranged in a neat row, are miniature plastic bottles of Bath & Shower Gel, Hand & Body Lotion, Shampoo & Conditioner, all with **Just For You** written on them.

It is the first time I have been alone since the car this morning and I have an uneasy sense of being watched on a screen.

I feel as if there are cameras on me as I take off the trench coat and throw it on the bed, plug the phone charger into a power point, attach the phone, fill the kettle with water from the sink in the bathroom, turn it on.

The phone begins pinging. Then a ringtone obliterates the noise of the kettle.

Tom calling . . .

It rings out and a red badge appears on MESSAGES. I access the voicemail.

—YOU HAVE THREE NEW VOICEMAILS.
—FIRST VOICEMAIL LEFT TODAY AT 18:42.
—*What the fucking hell are you playing at? Do you have any idea the shit show that you have caused? The children are traumatised. I had to ask Susan to come over. No matter what is going on this is selfish. Do you hear me? UNCONSCIONABLY FUCKING SELFISH. Phone me when you get this. Can you do me at least that courtesy?*

I delete the next two voicemails without listening to them, turn off the kettle, open the duty-free vodka and take a good long swig.

In the bathroom I undress, step into the shower. As it runs, the water becomes hotter and more forceful, blinding and deafening me while I rub Shampoo & Conditioner *just for me* through my short hair.

I feel I have no identity now, no point of reference.

Is this what I wanted? An expanse of nothing opening up where a future should be?

The white towels have a laundromat smell. I dry my hair with one, use two more on my body, then brush my teeth. There is red on one of the towels. My shin, where I bashed it on the step at the railway station, is bleeding, but not heavily. I stick a piece of toilet paper on the cut.

Naked, I wander back to the bedroom and stare into the full-length mirror. Stretch marks. Stomach slightly distended. Pubic hairs greying. Cellulite on bottom. Veins on hands. Wrinkles on neck.

For the last twenty years, I have been unable to see myself when I look in a mirror. What I see is a decline from a previous 'image' of myself and the need for improvement.

I 'need' to tone my stomach muscles. I 'need' to do something about my pubic hair. My teeth 'need' to be bleached again. Also, the frown line between my eyebrows is re-emerging since my last Botox treatment (to look more 'fresh'). And that sag on my jawline, either side of my chin (for which there is no remedy other than cosmetic surgery), is getting more pronounced.

For the last twenty years, I have been living as my own self-improvement project.

But I feel no need for improvement tonight.

Charming older men are 'silver foxes', but flirtatious middle-aged women are 'cougars'. Or, as my mother used to say, 'mutton dressed as lamb'. To be an older woman is to be fair game for ridicule. Your desire can be held against you, or worse, turned into a joke.

I am tired of being called a large cat or an old sheep or a female dog.

I take another mouthful of vodka. Then I get dressed, but don't bother with a bra. My shin is sore, but I ignore it. With the tweezers I bought earlier, I pluck a dark hair from my chin, rub some Hand & Body Lotion on my face, run my fingers through my still-damp hair.

I want to get out of the room, away from the phone, have another drink, and – even though I haven't had one since I met Tom – a cigarette. Between me and the night ahead, the delimitation is no longer solid.

I twist the two gold bands back and forth on my wedding finger, one plain, the other with an inset diamond, and slide them down into the palm of my right hand.

I hold them for a moment or two, and then put them in the drawer with the locked-down hairdryer.

The skin on my finger where the rings were is blanched white, like paper.

In the Hotel Bar-cum-Breakfast Room, I order a double vodka and white lemonade.

Donegal guy is sitting with his back to me, chatting to an older man. He doesn't turn round, but I know that he sees me. There is no one else in the bar except the girl serving the drinks, who looks about fourteen. The mahogany-haired woman's daughter, or granddaughter?

I knock back the vodka. I order another one, along with a pack of Marlboro Gold and a box of matches, and take them out with me to the smoking area. My trench coat is open, but I don't feel cold. I rest the glass on a metal keg while I open the Marlboro, take one out, light it, inhale deeply into my lungs. The taste burns my palate, but there is something pleasing about the look of the cigarette in my hand. Halfway through, I throw the stub away, swallow a mouthful of vodka.

WARNING: Tobacco smoke can harm your children.

I think of my father smoking in our old Ford Cortina, me in the back beside my brother, my mother in the passenger seat listening to the radio.

There is a creaking noise and the Donegal guy appears through a side door, announcing himself with a whistle that strikes me as gauche. He stands with his legs wide apart, his work boots covered in muck.

—How you gettin' on?

The accent is attractive, but in the light of the overhanging bulb, it is the best thing about him. His teeth are bad and his eyes are glassy from drink. His brown hair looks dusty. I stare at him until he is unable to control the colour rising in his face.

I light another cigarette, hold out the packet towards him. He takes one and I notice his fingers are scarred. I offer him the cigarette out of my mouth to light his.

The air is thick now with energy passing between us and out into the sky.

When I speak next my voice is different. The vowels are slimmer, the pitch higher.

—Your room or mine?
He takes a drag on his cigarette, laughs. He is uncertain now.
—Are you serious?
—Perfectly serious.
—Yeah, well, I . . .

Donegal guy is hooked.

—You will have to shower first.
He tries again to laugh but doesn't manage it.
—Are you ser—?
—And nothing weird, and I want to come first.

He takes another drag, exhales. He looks at me curiously.

—You're a mad bitch. Do you know that?
—Do we have a deal?
—Well, yeah . . . You're on, aye.
—Your room. OK?

—I suppose.

—What number?

—No number. I'm around the back in one of the prefabs.

—OK. You go ahead of me. Have a shower. Give me ten minutes. And leave your door open.

—All right.

I hear him call after me

—YOU'RE A MAD BITCH.

I go back inside. The wine-carpeted stairs are wavery. I am not drunk, but my step is high and jerky, like a marionette. In my room I brush my teeth again, go to the toilet, run my fingers through my hair and leave without looking at my phone.

Outside the temperature has risen and in the mild night air, I am sober again, sure-footed on the gravel. At the back of the hotel, a silver security light illuminates a row of prefabricated boxes. The door to one is open.

Inside, there's an unmade double bed, a pile of dirty laundry in the corner, a sink area covered in used mugs, a kettle, a box of teabags, a microwave cooker and a clutter of empty bottles and cans by a bin with no lid. Also, a mass-produced coffee table covered in stacks of coins and on the walls, more seascapes in cheap frames, and surprisingly a cheese plant in the corner in a too-small pot.

There must be a separate shower room, but I can't see it.

Warm air wafts from a slim storage heater.

Donegal guy is sitting on the bed, with a green towel around his waist. His hair is wet. I sit beside him. As I undress, he tells me the prefabs are cheap to rent. That all the young fishermen live in them, mostly sharing, some of the Vietnamese guys four or five to a room. He tells me that he is thinking of renting a flat . . . thinking of emigrating to Australia . . . thinking of retraining to be a tree surgeon . . .

While he is talking, I undress with complete ease. And it is more than the loss of inhibition from the vodka. My brain is not making any effort to conceal some part of my body.

Even with my husband, I always pulled in my stomach getting out of the shower.

I grow weary of Donegal guy's nervous chatter, kiss his mouth, remove the towel.

No more thinking.

His chest, back, thighs are white and cold as marble. His cock, too, is cold and smooth in my hand.

There is an odour from the bedsheets, and they ruck under me, their bobbled texture chaffing my skin. Donegal guy is perspiring in his groin and under his arms, but his sweat is clean, like seawater.

He kisses my breasts, pushes two fingers inside me. I tell him to stop, and he does. I explain that I want him to go down on me. I want him to put his tongue on my clitoris, and at the opening of my vagina.

He nods that he understands.

I lie back and think about a buxom woman in see-through red panties and high heels.

Thinking about the woman in see-through panties, arranging her in different positions, and imagining her begging for cock, while a tongue flicks back and forth across my clitoris and in and out of my vagina, I experience an intense orgasm.

Donegal guy is pleased.

We fuck for a bit and then he comes by jerking onto my bottom. Almost immediately, he jumps up, grabs a roll of kitchen towel from beside the sink and wipes himself.

—There's no booze but I can make you a cup of tea, if you like?
—What a gentleman . . . I'll have water.

My throat is dry.

He fills a chipped mug with water from the tap and tells me he has to be up at four.

I take a few sips.

—Will you not be exhausted?
—Nah, I'm used to it.

I ask him if it is true that all the fish are disappearing.

—Nah, it's totally fucked, like. The skippers do what they want and so long as there's no baby seals lying around or dead dolphins, nobody gives a fuck.

Later, Donegal guy gives my thigh a friendly slap, turns away from me, breathes heavily as he sleeps.

I move closer to him to stay warm, but I know I have to leave soon. Otherwise, I'll still be here when he returns tomorrow, the bed made, the room tidied, a bottle of wine open, and some Chicken Stupid Masala ready meal in the microwave.

I can smell socks from the pile of laundry, and stale alcohol from around the bin.

I slip out of the bed, put on my clothes and runners without tying anything, open the thin wallboard door, leave. A security light comes on, throwing shadows on the gravel.

— *We're sieving the last gold out of the river.*

Did I hear him say this or is it a line from a poem?

The hotel fire door opens onto a narrow door-lined corridor, along which the carpet releases a chemical odour that smells like fish. I cannot find my room. I turn right, then left, but each corridor replicates the next. The walls are decorated with safety certificates, fire extinguishers, framed prints of seascapes, and small domed cameras, like Greek evil eyes. I am at the point of banging on doors or shouting, when I finally see the steel numbers 4-and-1.

Inside the room, I check twice that the door is locked. How quickly we make things our own, turn them into territory we are prepared to defend.

Street light is coming in through the window, but I don't pull the curtains.

One more vodka. Then a shower, bed.

It is almost a plan.

But instead I pull my phone from its charger, touch the Home button.

There are ribbons of WhatsApp messages on the phone. Without opening it, I read one from Lauren:

—*So gone off to find yourself wtf*

In all, there are eleven missed calls: eight from Tom, one from Elaine, one from Susan, and one from the administrator of a school art competition.

The first new voicemail is Elaine.

—No matter what has happened we all love you—

DELETE.

No doubt she composed it after phoning her husband to make sure the children did NOT eat anything sugary before bed.

Then Susan.

—If you want to talk, I am—

DELETE.

Her husband will be down on his knees praying that I never, ever want to *talk* to Susan.

The phone rings while I'm holding it.

Tom calling . . .

I press Silent and sit on the edge of the bed, watching his name coming and going on the screen, lighting up and blacking out. It is almost comforting.

There is still some vodka in the bottle, but the taste now is oily and viscous. And the water pipes are gurgling. Nearby, somebody must be taking a shower or flushing the toilet.

I turn on the TV and leave the news channel running at low volume. Protesters marching in a European city. Riots in America. Floods. Wildfires. War. A row in the royal family . . .

In the shower, I let the water run for a long time.

—You're an idiot, my mother told me when I was nineteen. I had just done a pregnancy test in the bathroom.
—A complete idiot. What did you expect going back to his house drunk?

And I was a total and utter idiot to even think about keeping the baby.

And in the abortion clinic in London I was yet another Irish fucking idiot.

It was only when I met Tom and he wanted to marry me that I stopped feeling like an idiot.

I was sharing a house in Drumcondra with two nurses at the time, working in a shoe shop but calling myself an artist.

One night at a gig, I got chatting to a man who was wearing a suit where everyone else was wearing jeans. I was a bit drunk and when some dude started hitting on me, I mouthed to the man in the suit *rescue me*. Another one-night stand I thought at the time, but fast-forward a few weeks, and he *had* rescued me.

When Tom called to our house in Drumcondra and saw a hairdryer wedged in a chair, drying a pair of nylon tights, and an ashtray on the arm of the couch, overflowing with butts, he was shocked, but we laughed about it later, after I had said yes, I would move in with him.

Were we happy then? When I left the shoe shop to do the H.Dip. in Education? When I learnt to drive? When we got engaged? Married? Bought our first house? Had the children? Moved to a bigger house?

Yes.

But it was the kind of happiness where you think you're going to keep getting happier, so you don't pay much attention to it.

On weekends, in those early months of living together, when Tom got up before me to make breakfast in the mod-con kitchen, I remember lying in bed, staring out at the dull, overcast Dublin morning, pinching myself that anyone could be this 'happy'.

Money is the great antidote to shame.

—He's not your type, Elaine told me.

But he was funny and kind and he had a chequebook and a car, and he knew about cheese and wine and spoke French.

And the sex was good.

What did *he* see in *me*? Someone to rescue?

'Happily married' is not suddenly replaced by 'unhappily married'. There is a long interim period.

When the kids were about seven and five, I booked a family break for the Easter holidays, a package in a luxury hotel in the west of Ireland.

> *Complementary activities including yoga and whiskey tasting.*
> *Younger guests will be kept busy at our fun kids club.*
> *Spacious family suite complete with entertainment system.*

I quickly filled out the forms, gave my bank card details, pressed Book Now.

And then I sat there. Waiting.

But there was no pleasure. No satisfaction. No anticipation. No gratification. No fulfilment. No joy. No contentment. Just my inbox filling with additional special offers for spa treatments and day trip suggestions.

I felt like a receptor waiting for a dopamine hit that would never arrive.

I could hear the children fighting over the remote control in the living room, then the blare of a cartoon theme tune.

I opened a bottle of wine, poured a large glass, put a frozen pizza in the oven.

When Tom came home that evening we ordered food from a Thai restaurant, opened another bottle of wine, told each other how much we needed a break, how much fun it would be for the children, and how we should Take a Break more often.

When the phone lights up next, I answer it.

—Hello.
There is a long pause at the other end. And then, Tom.
—What the fucking hell are you playing at? he demands. I was about to phone the Guards.
Another long pause.
—Where are you?
And then.
—Have you any idea how selfish you are being? I had to—
I cut him off, speak as calmly as I can.
—I sent a message telling you that I was going away for a short while. I am perfectly safe and will be home soon.
He groans.
—Where the fuck are you? Can you at least tell me that? What kind of fucking game do you think you are playing? I really don't need this now. Whatever you think you are doing, you need to get home now. RIGHT NOW. Are you listening?

I hang up.

The bottle of vodka is nearly empty. I drain it in one mouthful.

I send another text message to Tom saying I am safe and well and will be in touch soon. Then I turn off my phone.

There is a scream from outside. A cat or a fox?

I go to the window and look out.

Everything is black. The sky. The clouds. The rain beating against the glass of the window.

And I am black, charred all the way through to the centre.

I have a vision of a torpid night, full of wreck and carnage. Everywhere slob lands and an iron-flat sea, the detritus of industry, cranes, waste plants, deformed metallics cluttering up the horizon, people pushing shopping trolleys and driving SUVs, buying happiness and earning money to buy more happiness, each one a dot on an ant hill globe, where lights go on and off, computers power up and down, and the only sounds are alarms and sirens and Siri and Alexa and people saying 😊 while they watch their kids on cameras and post photos of food on Instagram and forget to ever look at trees.

A security light comes on.

And there she is again in the glass of the window, that woman with short hair, but a Picasso painting now, features skewed and in the wrong place. With her off-kilter mouth, she accuses me of DRAMA, of making it all up about Tom and Elaine and my children and my mother. Of manufacturing my own unhappiness. Turning myself into a victim in some reality TV show.

A surge of vomit.

But I make it to the toilet.

The last food I ate comes out in the bowl exactly as it went in – lettuce, ham, slices of tomato – but now in a reddish jus.

I lie down on the bed, just for a minute.

If I have been seeking the moment when a limit is reached, when there is nothing ahead but chaos, I have found it.

If you lose one boundary, you lose them all.

Last August, when Lena first mentioned her plan to throw a party, I nodded in a *that sounds great* way, although I had no intention of going.

But those last few days of that month were strange.

Without warning my son turned up at the cottage with a girl called Órlaith who had a car. An old Micra. They were on their way to a music festival. She was a large girl with a nose ring and tattoos and was chatty, wanting to know all about the hens, the garden, the dog. It made things easier. When they were leaving, I hugged my son for a long time, my arms reaching all the way up his T-shirt to his shoulder blades.

In the aftermath of the visit, my skin was thin, as if the barrier between it and the world had dissolved and anything could get in, anything could get out. My routine collapsed and I started sleeping in the afternoons, ignoring the garden, leaving ellipses at the end of my thoughts. And sex came back. I masturbated in the bath at night, my body so porous that shame floated from it as light as dust motes.

And then the hen died and I disposed of it, threw on a dress and a pair of flip-flops and cycled out into the electric night air of August to Lena's party.

We were in the garden drinking red wine and listening to a cheesy Spotify mix and passing around a joint, when I realised the sky was black. No moon. No stars. Lena had put a string of lights like fireflies in the trees and I remember thinking how loose space was, so much of it a vacuum.

Then Lena started dancing. The sudden rupture of intimacy in seeing another body move so sensually was elating and I wondered about what it would be like to sleep with Lena. Her beauty, laughing and touching her hair in the firelight, almost broke me.

But then a friend of hers, a man called Izaak, starting telling me about his organic farm and the spell was broken. He promised to give me liquid seaweed for my rhubarb.

Breakfast Room

When I wake in the hotel room, my head feels as if a small metal plate has been inserted into my skull and is bearing down on my eyes. My mouth is dry, my neck stiff and aching. I pull back the bedcovers, put my feet on the carpet. In the pocket of my trench coat, I find the painkillers I bought before getting on the train and swallow them down with water from the tap in the bathroom. There is a bitter taste as they fragment at the back of my throat.

Through the window, the sky is roughed-up grey, and crows are gathering on telegraph wires. At ground level the trees are dark and brackish, the grass wet.

I watch my reflection in the glass as though it might suddenly burst into flames.

The room is overheated, but the window is designed not to open fully. The hotel car park is smaller than it seemed in the dark. To the left, the town, and beyond that the sea and cliffs. To the right the view is blocked by what looks like a fish processing plant.

My stomach is protesting in hard gassy knots against the painkillers.

In a driveway of a new-build house across the road, a father is loading a station wagon. He has a collection of bags, a briefcase, a fold-up travel cot, a baby in a portable car seat and a girl of about two. The baby is easily deposited in the front passenger seat, but the two-year-old won't play along. The father stoops down to button up her anorak, but when he tries to pick her up, she kicks out, scrunches up her face, begins to cry.

—*Have you any idea how selfish you are being?*

I get dressed, wipe the vomit stains from the toilet, switch on the tiny kettle, make a cup of tea with two sachets of sugar and four cartons of UHT milk, drink it while staring at the TV screen. It's too early to leave the hotel.

In daylight the breakfast room has a tiled floor and magnolia painted walls. Pine tables and chairs. In a corner, a plastic high chair. Fire alarm. Smoke alarm. A **NO SMOKING** sign. Framed Health & Safety certificates. The obligatory seascape prints. There is no trace of the bar. It has been transformed. The counter is now a buffet table. The low lighting is now bright. The bar-stools have been cleared away and replaced with pine tables and chairs.

A woman in a work suit is piling up a plate at the buffet counter. I wait for her to leave and then make straight for the **ORANGE JUICE MACHINE**. On top of the plastic contraption is a metal basket of oranges and inside it, a cog system through which the fruit rotates before being squashed. I fill a glass, drink it down in three gulps, refill the glass.

On each table there is a bowl of sugar sticks, a pair of wooden salt and pepper pots, a wicker basket of condiments and a fake Bonsai tree.

A girl, about seventeen, her hair dyed pink, is clearing a nearby table. She asks if I would like tea or coffee?

—Tea, please.
—You can get toast, bread, pastries at the buffet counter.
—Thank you.

From the kitchen there is a loud rattle of plates and the smell of toast.

 —But I can take your order if you'd like a cooked breakfast?
I am grateful for the warmth in her voice.
 —Yes, thank you. Some bacon. And scrambled eggs.

I am suddenly starving.

A couple with small children arrive in the entrance to the Breakfast Room. The mother jiggles a crying baby while she instructs the father to fetch the highchair, to seat the other children at a table, to ask the staff to heat some baby food. She has her make-up on and delivers her instructions in a calm, proficient tone. Only her eyes betray her, they are burnt-out.

In the hotel room, I think about having another shower, but I cannot bear the thought of undressing again. I put the empty vodka bottle into the plastic bag and throw the mints and travel toothbrush in the bin. I unplug the phone charger from the power point.

I have no missed calls. No voicemail.

The mother in the breakfast room is a good mother. But what if she slips up, even once, and hits her children or screams at them or bangs the door in their faces or leaves them with a negligent babysitter or rows with her husband in front of them or verbally abuses them or sometimes wishes she never had them? Is she then a bad mother?

Only women artists tell stories about motherhood that allows for ambivalence. Barbara Longhi with her painting of a mother reading a book while holding her baby. Or Del Kathryn Barton's painting of a stern mother and her three miserable children. Or Cecile Walton. That chilly scene of a mother in bed with a newborn, her breasts exposed, an older child looking anxiously on.

In the service station coffee shop I had noticed a mother feeding her baby, a nursing cover draped over her breasts. She looked calm, content even. I had not enjoyed breastfeeding my children. I did it for exactly six weeks as recommended, then switched to formula. I prided myself on doing things 'properly' with my children. Balanced diet. Restricted TV. Innovative birthday parties. Educational Christmas presents. But I was rarely content, often not calm.

—No, not like that, I said to my husband, early on, when he was struggling to change a nappy. Here, let me do it.

But all I ever hear is the story of The Mother Whose Children Are the Most Important Thing In Her Life.

Ask a mother how she is and more often than not she will tell you:

—The eldest, he's graduating next month and thinking of getting a place of his own . . . I'll miss him terribly of course . . . and my youngest, she's doing the Leaving Certificate this year . . . we're all on eggshells, sure you know yourself . . .

I remember pulling my son off me when he was two to leave him in the crèche, then crying when I sat back in the car, relieved to be free of him.

There is no alternative, I told myself.

Was that the truth?

Yes.

But it felt like a lie.

Perhaps because it was also true that a lot of the time I performed the role of Good Mother, not just for my children, but for society. I was afraid, not of failing, but of being seen to fail. The worst thing possible for a woman is to be considered a BAD mother.

And to this fear I sacrificed a real connection with my children. Whenever they did anything that might reflect poorly on my parenting – Lauren wanting to get a tattoo when she was fourteen, Mark bunking off school in Transition Year – I used withdrawal of affection (and later money) to bring them back 'on track'. Letting them know that the Mother Love they were in receipt of was conditional on their being obedient and successful.

How deep that shock must be buried.

Whatever I thought my children should learn – music, art, drama, football, French, how to bake a loaf of bread – I sent them to classes and paid someone to teach them. And when they were not at the crèche or Montessori or school or classes or activities, I arranged playdates for them, or took them to play centres or playgrounds or parks.

That simple joy of being with them, I lost it.

Or I allowed myself to lose it.

Now I would like nothing more than one more day with three-year-old Mark, even one more hour. To be back in a world of stars and moons and space rockets, with his obsession with trucks and the colour blue and the physical sensation of water, with his range of emotions that ran from delight to rage, nothing in between.

I remember how the three of them used to look in bed. Tom exhausted, his mouth open, Lauren tucked in tight beside him, Mark asleep on his chest. Around then was the last time I thought seriously about art, about how I might try to capture this mystery of the ordinary.

In twenty-first-century Ireland, there are plenty of stories that mothers can now publicly tell.

About menorrhagia, abortion, postpartum depression, endometriosis, menopause . . .

But even in the twenty-first century, there are still stories that mothers in Ireland cannot publicly tell.

> That they dislike one of their children.
> That they are bored with their 'nice' husband.
> That one day, while the 'nice' husband is out walking the dog, they check the search history on his laptop and find that he has been keeping company with 'legal teens'.
> That they are sometimes scared of their son.
> That their daughters blackmail them emotionally.
> That occasionally they think about killing themselves.

No one wants to hear these stories. Not her sister or her best friend, and certainly not the other women at the school gate. If a mother wants to tell one of these stories, she will have to pay someone to listen.

Sometime that night of the party, I got a desire to tell Lena the story about leaving the house in the suburbs and never coming back. I was drunk, but not so drunk that I didn't know what I was risking. I thought it would take ages to tell the story, to find a beginning, to settle on an end, but it was over in a few minutes.

But then, to tell a story is always to reduce it.

Lena was so quiet, I thought she must be asleep. But she wasn't asleep because she jumped up, saying we needed another drink, and returned with a bottle of pretend champagne and two flutes. While she chatted about her plans to build a summerhouse in the garden, I sat there sipping my drink, staring into the red ashes of the chimenea, feeling leavened, peaceful as though a butterfly that had been stuck in my stomach for years had just flown free.

When we finally fell asleep lying on a picnic blanket on the grass, I had one of those dreams where you fall off something, a curb or a platform, and my body must have jerked, because I felt her arm stretch around me in the darkness.

When I got home the next day, I swept the chicken coop, put down fresh straw, cleaned out the feeding trough and filled it with meal. Around me the hens clacked in a tone that suggested that this was the least I could do. Then I stripped my bed and put a wash on. Later, when I hung the sheets out, I expected them to dry quickly in the late summer heat, but around lunchtime the sky clouded over, and a whole month of rain fell in an hour. Afterwards the water in the tap was rust-coloured and I had to boil it before drinking. And later the electricity went again. I had already started stocking up on candles for winter and storing water.

These days, I see the signs of breakdown everywhere. Inside people, in their families, in communities, in society, in the planet.

Like everyone else, I spent most of my life pretending that I couldn't see them. It was easier that way. Easier to take the cat to the grooming salon and plan sun holidays and lay cobble loc in the driveway and worry about food intolerances and fall asleep in bed at night with Netflix playing on a giant wall-mounted TV.

The day after the day after the party I was depressed. Between my toes was raw from dancing in cheap flip-flops and my head still ached. I felt I had been a fool to tell Lena about leaving the house in the suburbs, and the hens were agitated. I chucked handfuls of meal at them like stones, took some Panadol and went to bed. Around nine that night I registered the dog barking and got up, pulled the curtains and let the dog out, made a cup of tea while I waited for him to come back in, put some dog food in the bowl and went back to bed.

I didn't even brush my teeth.

Later, around midnight, 'out of the blue' I charged a Nokia phone Lena had given me and called my husband. I remembered the number. But before the ringtone even sounded I understood that this was a compulsion, and not desire.

He answered straight away, although my number must have displayed as unknown and the national code as UK. Maybe he guessed that it was me. Maybe he had a UK-based client.

 —I am sorry, I whispered.
There was a long pause.
 —Yeah? he asked finally.

Where did this new manner of speaking come from, I wondered. Next, I thought, he will be saying, For sure . . .

I was about to say again that I was sorry when he spoke.

 —There is a solicitor's letter in the post.
 —OK, I said.

And then he said goodbye.

I thought of adding, Give my love to the children. But I didn't.

I hung up.

There was a tight, grating feeling in my chest as though something was eating at my heart.

But it was just loneliness.

Some days I thought I might drown in it, but most days it just sat in my chest, not bothering me too much. And sometimes I even forgot about it altogether for hours, days, a week.

I know now that it will always be there.

Bus

In my room, I would like to get back into bed and sleep, stay in the hotel for another night or two, maybe even hook up with Donegal guy again.

But I *need* to make decisions.

I finish dressing and go downstairs.

There is no one at the reception desk and the rebarbative sound of vacuuming is making me feel sick again. The mahogany-haired woman passes by carrying towels, but makes no sign of recognition. Finally, the girl with pink hair appears.

—Checking out?
—Yes.
She takes my key card, tells me, in a Welsh accent, to have a good day.

At the far side of the hotel, weeds sprout between flagstones and a few premature snowdrops struggle in a grass verge. Along the gable wall, three large bins are lined up. Blue, brown and green. I chuck the empty vodka bottle in the nearest one, and continue down the hill, taking a local road to my right which is signposted for the harbour.

It is colder nearing the harbour, but the salty air is making me feel less dead. A strong wind comes in off the sea, tugging at the fishing boats by the pier, and the waves are foamy and grey on the small, pebbled beach. Further out there is a heavy mist. And overhead, the alarm of almost invisible seagulls.

There are red notifications on the screen of my phone, but I ignore them.

What now?

Phone Tom?

Get the ferry back to Ireland?

Take some paid sick leave from work and pretend that none of this has happened?

'Today's news is tomorrow's fish and chip paper.' Another one of my mother's favourite sayings.

The harbour here has long since fallen into desuetude. Precast concrete slabs laid end-to-end form a wall that is stained black in patches and splattered with bird droppings. The sea slaps non-stop against the wall's flanks, and beneath it the gangway is littered with pillars and bollards and the detritus of fishing.

On the small pebble beach, plastic bags and plastic wrappers, plastic cups and plastic bottles, plastic spoons and plastic straws, and a dead dogfish with seaweed trailing from its jaw.

My heart is beating too fast inside my trench coat.

But there is something else. Some sadness that I have been carrying for a long time, telling myself that everything would be 'fine'.

It won't be fine.

When I was young I read in a library magazine that within a century all the coal on Earth would be burned and that all the crude oil would be exhausted. I remember that for a time afterwards I walked around in a daze, thinking it strange that everyone kept shovelling coal into fires and pumping petrol into cars. And then I forgot about it.

Until now.

Now, it has all become strange again.

You think that it is *you* that is breaking down – *your* family, *your* community, *your* society – but it is the whole world, and the sadness I've been carrying around is about this new reality that nothing – not even nature – is immune from breaking down.

On the steps leading to the jetty, a pair of crows squabble over an empty chip bag.

Nearer the boats, there is a rumble of activity and I turn back. Like the truckers on the ferry, this is a world of men. I have no desire to encounter Donegal guy in daylight, to catch snatches of laughter on the air.

In the village I sit on a bench in a small park.

A strange fugue state has overtaken me now and everything seems lifeless, foggy. Around me people seem like robots, or figures from a dream. I know I have emotional connections to my husband, my children, my best friend, my dead mother, but some synapse in my brain is stuck, or broken, and I cannot access emotions, only observe them, as you observe clouds passing by in a calm sky. I don't want to think. What I want to do is stay sitting here, motionless, like the roots of a great tree deep in the earth.

A man with a bulbous nose is kicking a ball around the grass with his son, aged about five. He shouts at his son to run faster, kick harder, but the boy is chubby and slow and keeps missing the ball. The boy's mother turns up and throws me a suspicious look. She thinks she has something I might want.

I take out my phone. Six WhatsApp messages, two missed calls, four text messages.

I tap the green WhatsApp icon and read a new message from my son:

—*please come home*

Rain begins to fall. At first paper thin, then heavier. All colour is drained from the sky.

I stroll the rest of the way to the village trying again to think, *What next?*

In a corner shop, I drift around the aisles, picking up a bottle of 7UP, a bar of chocolate, more mints. There is a milky coating on my teeth and I have the taste of cigarettes in my mouth.

In the shop's porch, while I am waiting for the rain to ease, and wondering about the ferry schedule back to Ireland, I see a faded handwritten ad on a Community Noticeboard.

Holiday cottage to rent, quiet location, two miles from ▮▮▮▮▮▮ £150pw

That is cheap, I think, and on impulse I unpin the ad from the corkboard, put it in my jeans pocket. Then I return to the shop to buy an umbrella. The woman at the till is silent as I tap my card again.

In strong wind, the umbrella packs in almost immediately, inverting itself and buckling. I am tempted to chuck it in a hedge, but instead I poke it into the narrow aperture of a bin, its spokes sticking out like spider legs.

As I walk back up the hill, my thoughts shoot everywhere.

For years now I have worked to eliminate free-flowing thought, keeping my brain engaged like a car with its accelerator constantly depressed. News on the radio in the morning. Headlines on my phone. More news in the car. At work the tabs on my desktop computer always open on shopping sites. In the evening, boxsets on the flat screen television in the living room. Another smaller TV in the den. And a wall-mounted one in the bedroom, where I usually fell asleep catching up on news headlines.

An SUV passes, splashing water on my runners and jeans. A surge of anger pulses through me, then dies away. I haven't the energy to maintain it.

I pass the driveway where I saw the father struggling with the two-year-old girl earlier. The grass on the front lawn is trim, but the garden next door to it is overgrown. Then I see the sign, almost obscured by the weeds: **WILDFLOWER MEADOW**.

When she was eighteen my daughter wanted us to dig up our front lawn and plant wildflowers to attract bees. Some houses in the estate had already done this, mounting signs on the gate or the wall in case anyone thought they had neglected to mow the grass. Uncharacteristically, my husband said NO, and a row started. Tom said that he'd read somewhere that the flowers mostly provided food for insects that are *not* threatened. But even Lauren knew the real issue for him was the unkempt appearance of the garden.

All those years spent getting the house done. Converting. Remodelling. Redecorating. Painting. Sanding wooden floors. Until there was no trace left of the original. What did I think? That if I got the house right, my life would be right? That if our home *looked* perfect, then we were a happy family?

Our cleaner, Anya, has worked for us for the last four years, vacuuming the house from top to bottom, every Tuesday.

I am sorry now that she will always remember me as a bitch.

The last time I saw Anya was when I was off work with a head cold. She was mopping the floor in the hall, wearing a man's check shirt to protect her clothes, her dark hair pinned up. The wine glasses had just come out of the dishwasher streaked instead of sparkly, and I was on a rant about the short lifespans of appliances when I saw her sort of shrug. Then she stopped mopping and looked at me.

—It is fixed before too long, no?

I wanted to slap her.

Did Anya say she was Bulgarian? I think so, but I'm not sure. Was she married, single, divorced? Gay or straight? Did she have children? Where did she live? I never asked.

I am already thinking of Anya in the past, though she will probably continue to clean the house every Tuesday.

Whether I am there or not, everything will go on.

The rain has eased, but I step into a bus shelter where an old man and a teenage girl are waiting for a bus. She has a ring in the septum of her nose and the old man's coat is frayed at the cuffs. Beneath the plexiglass, there is a faded bus timetable, a poster for the Samaritans and another for a product or a service whose name has been daubed over with spray paint, but whose tagline remains visible.

THE FUTURE IS FLEXIBLE

I am tired and hungover and my lower back is nagging, but I do not want to get back on the ferry and return to the house in the suburbs. Not yet. Nor do I want to return to the hotel, check in again, the mahogany-haired woman pretending she doesn't recognise me. What I want is to be alone, to think. I take the noticeboard ad from my pocket, tap the number on the keypad of my phone.

It goes straight to voicemail:

—The number you have . . . cannot be . . . after the tone . . .
I panic, blurt out what sounds like a string of disconnected phrases.
—Ad in shop ... cottage to rent ... one week, two at most ... thank you.
I hang up.

There is a thin red bench in the bus shelter and I sit down, suddenly weak and overcome by a mild torpor.

Along the road, tattered leaves, stunted trees planted in concrete, a hedgerow with tiny, atrophied berries. A single enormous jackdaw crosses the sky.

Last weekend my husband needed his black linen shirt to wear to a drinks party some client was hosting. When he found it in the ironing basket, he went through the motions of opening presses, asking in a mock American accent:

—Where's the iron kept these days, honey?
—Here, I said to him finally, let me do it.

First I reversed the button band and ironed along it, then I turned the shirt over and ironed the left side, back, right side, shoulders, sleeves, collar. Then I did up the top button and put it on a hanger, stowing the iron away in the same press in the utility room where it is always kept. While I was doing this, I could hear the urgent commentary on a football match coming from the TV in the living room: turnover, left, right, pass, tackle, shot off. And then cheering. Someone had—

My phone is vibrating in the pocket of my trench coat.

On the screen there's an area code and number I don't recognise.

—Hello?
—Hello. You left a message. About the cottage . . .
—Yes. A week . . . or maybe two. Is that OK?
—When were you thinking?
—Today. Can I take it today?
—Today? All right, so. But there's been no one there since the summer.
—I came in on the ferry . . . at Fishguard, yes . . . but I have no car—
—The best thing to do is to take the bus. It's about a ninety-minute journey. I'll meet you at the Grand Hotel at half past three. I can drive you the rest of the way.
—Drive?
—It's less than half an hour.
—Yes. OK. Will I text you when I am on the bus? I have to check the times. Is that OK?
—That's OK.
—Does the house have a radio?
—A radio? We can sort something out . . .

I am aware that I should be feeling something as I wait for a bus to take me to a town whose name I can't pronounce to rent a cottage from a man whose name I don't know. But I feel nothing. It is all too unreal for feelings.

I am experiencing something, however. The faintest memory of something I have not experienced for decades, not since I left home to go to art college, maybe even further back than that.

Something like freedom.

A single-decker bus turns the corner, wends its way along the road, and hisses to a stop. Two young men turn up and push their way on first. Then the teenage girl. Then the old man. Then me.

I stumble over the name of the town I want to travel to, but from behind the protective glass, the driver nods without looking up, and I tap my card on a machine, collect a ticket.

At the back of the bus, I take a seat beside another that has ripped upholstery. The nearest passenger is a man with his hair cut in a tonsure sitting on a folding seat. A scar, in the bare part, is shaped like a dorsal fin. Opposite him a woman wearing a hijab is reading a 'celebrity memoir' by someone I have never heard of.

The bus stays sitting at the stop for ten more minutes with its heating on. The windows become clouded with steam and I consider taking my trench coat off, but my body wants to feel something protective around it. Inside my runners, my feet are damp.

Finally, the bus takes off and, for a while, the gyrations of the engine are comforting.

I look out as we leave the village and enter the countryside. More land in geometric shapes. Cows gathered in corners of fields. Trees and hedges and distant hills.

Then fog. I can see close up but have no depth of vision, it is erased in whiteness, fields trees hedges all washed out, everything disappeared in mist.

With nothing else to distract me, the questions start spiralling in my head.

—Where are you going?
—What are you doing?
—Are you crazy?

At the next stop, an old woman with a wheeled shopping bag sits beside me in the seat with ripped upholstery. She jostles her body against mine. There are dark hairs on her upper lip, the smell of unwashed human.

The driver has the radio on and I can hear the chorus of a song I never liked.

At one of the stops, an old stone church with granite pillars, lopsided with time.

On the motorway, we pick up speed and the scenery streaks by in a blur of green.

I have missed the opening of it, but something has started up between the tonsure man and the woman in the hijab.

I shut my eyes, pretending not to be aware. She seems to be giving as good as she's getting, though, and when he leaves the bus, a little later, it is with a torrent of impotent abuse.

All I want now is to get to the cottage and sleep.

I catch sight of my reflection in the window of the bus, and for a moment, I think I am looking at my mother. I am not unsettled by the resemblance, which surprises me.

After my father's death, she cut her hair short and took to wearing jackets not dissimilar to the trench coat I have on. The good wool coat, hanging in her wardrobe, was kept for special occasions, a trip to Wexford to visit her sister or a funeral. She was a tall woman. Taller than I am. Even slightly taller than my father in their wedding photographs.

As a widow, she worried about loss of respectability. A still-attractive single mother on a small pension could easily find herself the subject of gossip in a small Irish town, especially with no relatives to support her. She must have felt vulnerable. She must have worried about her children. Maybe that was why she behaved as she did when I was nineteen.

In the end, she died alone.

She had a stroke in February and spent three weeks in hospital. She returned to the nursing home afterwards, but never recovered.

Earlier that afternoon, two or three hours before she died, I had been at her bedside. But she had been asleep, waking only once to stare at me without any trace of recognition.

When the nurse had asked me to step outside while he emptied the catheter, I had taken it as an excuse to leave.

Later, when I got the phone call informing me of her passing, I was sitting at the island in my kitchen, most of the way down a glass of wine.

I brushed my teeth, got in the car and went straight back to the nursing home. She was still lying there, looking exactly as I had last seen her, but dead. I bent down and kissed her lips. Such a small thing for a child to give a parent. A kiss. But I had never done it, and as my lips touched hers, I realised that it did not matter anymore whether my mother's life had been happy or miserable. Her life had always been slipping away from her while she was searching for something to make her happy or trying desperately to avoid anything that might make her miserable. And now it was over.

Standing beside her, I felt uncomfortable. I didn't know what I was expected to do next.

I was relieved when the nursing staff took over. They were anxious to get the paperwork signed off and the undertakers in before the end of their shift.

As I left the nursing home, I noticed daffodils in pots and a cherry blossom tree in bloom along the driveway. And on the lawn, a small squat machine running up and down cutting the grass, its sensor lights flashing whenever it strayed too near the edge.

The funeral took place on an overcast morning in March. The sky was blank. The wind was biting but people kept saying how great it was that the rain had stayed away. I wore a designer black coat that I had bought in the January sales, with an occasion such as this in mind.

When I had broken the news of our mother's death to my brother, it was over an unstable internet connection, on a Skype call. He cried, but in the end he decided against travel. It was hectic with his business, he said. And anyway, he could watch the livestream of the funeral on YouTube, order a wreath to be delivered, post messages on the WhatsApp family group. Why make the time-consuming journey?

The screen had frozen then, and I had ended the call.

Through the viewing and the Mass and the burial and the meal in a hotel afterwards, I felt a strange giddiness, as though something exciting had happened. But all that had happened was that my mother had died.

It was a release, I told myself. And told everyone else I spoke to.

Lauren recited a poem from the altar. She wore a dark grey skirt and jacket that I had insisted on. I was annoyed, looking at her, that the blouse she had selected herself was a flimsy-looking thing.

Dressed in a smart navy suit, Mark gave a separate reading. I had practised it with him, but he still faltered in the delivery.

And then it was over.

And I went back to work.

It was nearly Easter by then and there was a new palette of yellow and green in the verges of the dual carriageway as I drove towards the city in the mornings. Each evening was brighter for a few minutes longer than the one before. The whole world sloping towards summer.

I never asked my mother what she thought or felt about anything. I had no interest in what she thought or felt about anything. Years before, I had given her a pass grade as a mother and awarded myself an 'A' for being a good daughter. That was how I wanted it.

After she died I went through the old photographs she had kept in a box in her wardrobe at the nursing home. My brother wanted me to send him copies of them. I thought that this would take ages. But it didn't. In the box, there were only fifty-two photographs. Nine of me. Fifteen of him. Twenty-eight of us together. The earlier ones with my mother also in the frame.

Maybe that was why it was more emotional than I had expected. The sparseness of the photographs. How badly taken so many of them were.

Sometimes I wish I was back in that hospital room with her, treasuring her thin hair and pallid face, the lightness of her bones. And for everything else – all the trivia and petty grievances – to be gone. Only love left. What else is there? To hold her wrinkled hand and wet her lips with ice, kiss her forehead as she slips away.

I have thousands of photos of my own children, and hundreds of videos. New baby, cute toddler, first day in school, missing front tooth, blowing out birthday candles, first bike, visit to Santa, Christmas morning, school plays, holiday in France, sporting achievements, academic achievements, graduations, debs ball. *Everything* was photographed.

My memories of my children are memories of photographs.

The bus slows. Cars are waiting to join the long queue for a Drive-Thru Fast Food Outlet. On the outskirts of the town there are signs for a shopping centre and a hospital and a technical college. Then the bus crosses a bridge over a river and comes to a halt beyond a train station.

The driver shouts back to tell me that this is my stop.

The very old woman with the wheeled shopping bag is gone.

I hadn't noticed her getting off the bus.

The town is not dissimilar to towns in Ireland. More attractive, with Georgian buildings and a cobblestone Market Square. More neatly maintained. But still, a medley of fast food outlets wafting cooking oil through extractor fans, ladies boutiques, charity shops, pubs, bookmakers, heritage buildings with bins outside for cigarette butts, funeral homes, hair salons, a café with cats that you can pet. Everything tamed and manageable. Even the war memorial with its two flags.

I wonder if Wales is also a country that doesn't exist.

In the Ireland that doesn't exist, everyone ambles to the local pub in soft rain to drink stout and to listen to traditional music and to have the craic. Where society is secular and tolerant, and healthy young women and men play traditional sports in lush green fields and are hospitable to strangers and proud of their native language. Where life is easy-going and every second person is some class of poet.

I have seen this country on TV and read about it in books, but I have never lived there. I have lived only in a country obsessed with money. The earning of it, the spending of it, the stashing of it, the making it 'work for you', the bringing up of children who understand its 'value'.

I am tired of living in a country that doesn't exist.

I find a coffee shop – without cats to pet – and use the toilet. In a pharmacy next door I ask the assistant what cream is best to put on a deep cut. Inside my jeans, my shin has started to throb gently. She tells me they are all the same, so I buy the generic one and some cotton wool.

There is still an hour to kill before meeting the landlord.

Christmas lights are strung across the High Street and there are posters in windows already advertising **BLACK FRIDAY** and the **ARRIVAL OF SANTA** to his grotto in the shopping centre. I stop at an ATM machine and take out some cash, fold the notes into my wallet. On the pavement outside a Red Cross Charity Shop, a middle-aged busker is singing a Bob Dylan song.

—*The answer, my friend, is blowin' in the wind . . .*

Further away from the centre, **FOR SALE** signs decorate vacant terraced houses with iron security bars on the windows.

I turn down a side street.

At the entrance to a block of flats a man in shorts and slip-on shoes is drinking a can of coke. His shins are etched pink from scratching.

He says '*Nohs-dah*' and I say 'Hello' back.

Further up the street a new-generation EV is parked on a double yellow line and as I pass it an inferno of barking erupts from inside a boarded-up warehouse. At a chippers, teenagers push each other in horseplay or bullying. A row of pollarded trees, their leaves stripped bare, look ghoulish in lamplight and I retrace my steps back to the centre. The air is raw now and my leg is throbbing again.

The silence of the city streets. The blue air. The people on balconies smoking cigarettes, watching each other.

I am tired. In my eyes a sensation of metallic dust and my eyelids full of weight. Orange paper lampshades against black when I close them. Memory glimmers and hints but shows nothing clearly. It refuses to tell stories.

All I can recapture from the past is the boredom. Sometimes it felt as though my neck and arms and back had rusted from it, my brain, my guts, my heart. These last years, no matter what I did or where I went – even when I went to meet Elaine for lunch, or on yet another family holiday – I expected in advance to be bored.

It seems to me now that halfway through life is about the right time for women to feel RAGE. I know I did, eventually. With my husband, children, dead mother, best friend, good neighbour, a man in a van, a woman in a retail store, a guy at a frozen yogurt stand. I was so full of rage that I wanted to scream or to hit someone.

But the further away I get from the house in the suburbs, the more the past recedes into dream, until the only certainty is the impossibility of returning.

It is possible to step out of one life into another. But there is no going back.

At the Hot Food counter in the Convenience Store, the staff wear hair nets. I realise I am hungry and consider buying a cooked chicken, but the sight of so many rotating bronze carcasses puts me off. My eyes prefer strawberries and avocados, bunches of perfect yellow grapes. But I stick to basics: eggs, bread, ginger biscuits, tea, a tin of barista coffee, milk, butter, a jar of marmalade, soap, wash-up liquid, a two-pack of toilet paper. I know I am forgetting things but the wire basket is getting heavy, so I slip a bottle of wine in on top of the biscuits, make for the automated checkout machines.

PLEASE SCAN AN ITEM OR TOUCH THE SCREEN TO START

A queue has formed, so I duck sideways into the traditional checkout lane. I feel light-headed under the strip lighting. The woman in front of me – black trousers, a polycotton blouse, pumps worn down on one side – empties her basket onto the conveyer belt in groups:

> Tampons/budget firelighters
> Chocolate digestive biscuits/a tin of prunes
> Chilled pasta/a tub of arrabbiata sauce/a litre of slim milk
> A packet of little gem lettuce/a net of easy-peel oranges

She then hurries to the other side to pack.

—Can you be careful with that? she snaps.

The cashier – an older man with nails that are not clean – has dumped her firelighters down on top of the packet of little gem lettuce.

I chuck the contents of my basket onto the belt, pay and leave, the wine bottle clinking against the glass jar of marmalade inside my plastic bag.

The hotel where I've arranged to meet the landlord is a fine old Georgian building, a bit neglected now, with flaking woodwork and a PVC porch tacked on the front, an artificial Christmas tree twinkling in its window.

Inside, the bar is compact: a counter with stools, tables at a window, an alcove containing some slot machines and a dart board. The walls are painted a sanguine colour. Behind the counter there is an enormous gilt-framed mirror. I see my reflection in it as I order coffee and a sparkling water.

The barman is bald and has a tight sweater that shows his 'six pack' to full effect.

And the bar is well-stocked, especially with independent whiskey brands, all wall-mounted with optics.

I choose a table from where I can observe the main entrance.

The landlord sounded trustworthy on the phone, but I want to see him before he sees me.

My trench coat is damp and I drape it over a radiator, and resist a temptation to put my runners on the hot pipes that are running along the skirting board. I am overheated otherwise, but my feet are still cold.

In the alcove, a young couple display that weird performative energy of people on a Tinder date. An exaggerated laugh from her. Animal attentiveness from him.

There is no one else around.

A clock in the shape of a rugby ball shows that I have ten more minutes to wait. I consider charging my phone from a power point on the wall, but decide against it. I don't want to see missed calls and messages. I just want to be alone, to think. Just for a week or two. Is it really so much to ask?

My order arrives. The coffee is over-brewed but comes with a wrapped biscuit and a jug of milk. The bottle of sparkling water has been decanted into a glass of ice. I take a sip of the coffee, move on to the water.

The couple in the alcove are playing darts now. Very badly. She can barely manage to hit the board and he is not much better. But there's a lot of joking, laughing, touching.

Outside, tiny hailstones begin to fall. I hear them tinkling against the glass before I see them. They appear too frail to stick to anything, but they are persistent, on and on, until soon everything is coated in whiteness. Cars, pavement, road, shops. My eyes soften with tiredness. I would like to order a vodka, smoke a cigarette and melt away into some other life. The thought of having to make small talk with a stranger is filling me with dread.

When an old silver sedan pulls up across the road, I know immediately that it is him.

The man who gets out is about sixty, but sprightly, wearing corduroy trousers and a worn waxed jacket, boots. He has white hair, light and fluffy, and a pink complexion. He hunches for a moment against the wind, folds in the wing mirrors, says something to a dog in the back of the car, then bangs the door, turns the key, pads slowly through the hail towards the hotel.

I am standing out of my seat when he arrives, smiling.

—Hi, I greet him.

I tell him my name and remind him of our phone call.

His blue eyes settle on me for a moment, then flit away before returning, but I have caught the expression. He is relieved that I look 'normal'.

—How are you? Some weather out there.
His hand is out to shake my mine.
—Hello Huw. Nice to meet you.

He pulls out a chair and sits down. We exchange minimal personal information before chatting about the bus journey, the hailstones, how changeable the weather is these days. There is a liveliness in my voice that I did not expect and already I am adding grace notes of a Welsh accent to my own.

The barman comes to the table and the two men talk about a rugby match.

—Will you have a drink? Huw asks.
I hesitate, say no, sip my icy water.

He orders a whiskey I have never heard of, knocks it back straight.

—Right then, he announces.

I follow him out into the night.

Cottage

Outside, the hail has disappeared as suddenly as it appeared and my boots crunch across the street to the parked car. The air is freezing now.

Inside the old, battered sedan, a sheepdog starts jumping around. Huw unlocks the passenger door and I sit in, dumping the plastic bag of shopping at my feet. The back seats have been removed and there is a metal grid behind me, beyond it an array of tools, a bundle of logs, a pair of folded blue overalls, a canister of camping gas. And the dog, a Welsh Collie as it turns out, which gets excited again when Huw sits in.

Huw starts the engine, says '*Ndah-well*' a few times until the dog circles its body, avoiding the clutter, and settles down on an old, woollen blanket. The air from the heater smells of old tobacco.

Through the windscreen, the sky is laced with pink as dusk begins to fall.

After a short burst of information about the cottage, Huw falls silent. His body language betrays no curiosity about my circumstances and he drives without needing to have a relationship with the road, neither rancour nor pleasure, just passing over it, leaving no trace, as though driving were thought and not action. We turn left out of the town by the last of the houses, under a railway bridge, and out into the countryside. Each impression is overlaid by the next until grey sky seems to swallow up the whole scene.

At the edge of the upholstery on the driver seat, a punch hole with charred circumference, and hanging from the rear-view mirror, a red cardboard air freshener in the shape of a deer. The floor mats look new. There is a modest gold band on the ring finger of Huw's left hand. Wiry black hair pokes out from beneath the sleeve of his jacket.

Night is falling now.

Come, seeling night/Scarf up the tender eye of pitiful day . . .

No Irish person of a certain age ever forgets the Shakespeare they studied in school.

Further into the countryside, the road surface becomes harder. Or else the car's chassis is particularly thin. I don't know which. But the judder creates an atmosphere of intimacy. Heating blasts at my feet, making me sleepy and I wish we could drive forever along these dark curving roads, with the hedges flashing by, the houses and the inky silhouettes of trees, illuminated in headlights, all props from a dream.

My body is loosening, but not from alcohol. Tiredness, probably. And the thought of arriving at a place where I can be completely alone. Inside my boots, my feet have expanded with the warm air and the cut on my shin has stopped throbbing.

I am almost asleep when there's a loud THUD and a jolt to the wheel on my side.

Have we driven over something, killed something in the darkness?

But it is only a puncture.

Huw pulls in at the base of a driveway and asks me to stand out.

—The weight on the passenger side, you see.
—That's all right.
—It might knock it off the jack again.

The first thing I look at is not the damaged tyre, but the constellations overhead. Gold in the vast blackness. I don't know the names of any of them. Plough. That's about it. Funny to think that they are forever pushing away from each other.

Huw hands me a torch to hold while he fetches equipment from the boot and starts to raise the jack under the damaged tyre. The dog jumps out and disappears into hedges on the driveway. Huw curses in Welsh and interrupts his work to round him up again.

Cold is permeating my bones and I become aware of the menace of hedges beyond the range of torchlight. Wind creeps up behind me, rushes through my body.

In the pale beam, the man crouched in front of me looks older now, nearer seventy.

He snaps off the hubcap, loosens the nuts with the wheel brace, rolls the flat tyre away from the wheel, replaces it with the spare, returns the wheel nuts, lowers the car, and tells me to sit back in while he tidies everything into the boot.

When we get going again, the atmosphere is different. I root in the plastic bag, open the pack of toilet paper, unroll some and give it to Huw to wipe his hands. He doesn't know what to do with the blackened wad of paper afterwards and stuffs it into his jacket pocket.

—The wife will kill me when she finds that. Thirty-seven years we've been married. You wouldn't get as long for murder.

He laughs at the old joke.

And I laugh, too.

He tells me that the cottage belonged to his mother. That it had been in her family for generations. That she lived there all of her life. That she had wanted to die there but 'lost her marbles'. Quite suddenly, he explained. One week she was fine, the next she was walking the road late at night with only her nightdress on. Early onset dementia.

There is a long pause and then he adds.

—My father died years ago in a farming accident.

When I'm relaxed like this people tell me things.

—How did it happen? I wonder.

He glances across at me, then back at the road. It is obvious that no one has ever asked him this question, and I have no idea why I did.

Another long pause. I am about to apologise for intruding, when he speaks again.

—It wasn't an accident. He hanged himself in the barn.

I am annoyed that I have veered us into this territory, but I can't think of anything to say to get us back out, so I stay silent.

—The barn was demolished a few years after that. No sign of it now.

I try again to think of something to say, but nothing comes, and I let the conversation die. There is already too much between us now, invisible words haunting a cold November night.

I had thought of saying something to him about the small, terraced house where I grew up, about my father, about my mother. But that is a rule of the old life. Someone discloses something, you tell them something in return. All the unspoken deals, the need to balance the books.

Nonetheless, I imagine myself answering the unasked questions.

—Yes, I have been married for twenty-four years now.
—Yes, the BIG ANNIVERSARY next year.
—Two children.
—A girl of twenty-one at university.
—And a boy in his last year of secondary school.
—No, that's true.
—It is not always easy.
—Yes, it can be hard to keep the spark alive.

Even in my imagination, I don't add that what holds most marriages together is the unspoken agreement that nothing *new* will be introduced.

Of course, the 'spark' in most marriages is the new car or the new house or the new baby or the new job or the new investment or the new holiday home or the new family member or the new grandchild.

But never new OPINIONS or DESIRES or THOUGHTS.

Changing opinions or desires or thoughts while married is a form of infidelity. Which is why most married people who want new opinions or desires or thoughts often try to get them by having an affair.

But an affair rarely leads to much more than heartache or amusement. Or both. Which is why having an affair can be a great way of keeping a marriage going.

And there are many good reasons to keep a marriage going. Children. Finances. Companionship. Security. Even love.

But forty . . .

Fifty . . .
Sixty years . . .
It's a long time to live in close proximity with one other person.

If it is women that make their marriages into stories, it is men like my husband who believe them.

I imagine telling Huw about that holiday in France.

—I came back into the living room, I say, after pushing our daughter onto her bed and spitting into her face . . .

No, I can't imagine telling Huw about that holiday in France.

I came back into the living room after pushing my daughter onto her bed and spitting saliva into her face. Tom and Mrs Gorgeous were over by the record player listening to some jazz record, and I was watching her golden feet as they moved lightly back and forth, free of their espadrilles, no nail varnish, just bleached half-moon nails and a delicate silver anklet. Tom was riffing about jazz being the only really free music. I tried to make conversation with Mr Nice, asking him about work/travel/hobbies, while he made a valiant effort to unglue his eyes from his wife long enough to answer each of my questions.

The next morning, I was up first, opening shutters to let the sun in, clearing away bottles and dirty glasses, making crêpes and fresh orange juice for breakfast. Then the goodbyes began. Two-cheek kisses and promises to keep in touch, to get together again back in Dublin. And then, when they were finally gone, the most terrible emptiness.

I spent the rest of that day in bed, with Tom coming in at intervals to ask where Mark's hay fever medication was, where the suncream was, or what he should cook for dinner, and even at one point to say how tired he was before making to lie down on the bed beside me. I put my hand across the chenille bedspread and said NO and he just sloped away.

I tried to talk to Tom about it afterwards. But he preferred winning to talking.

I thought of leaving him after that holiday. I always thought of this when he was out of the house and I was in it, but then the kids, when they heard his key in the door in the evening, would always start

—DADDY! DADDY!

Over time I became too lazy to argue with Tom, to say what I felt, to even think about what it was I did feel.

But there was enough goodwill between us to keep going, and over time, with the arrival of grandchildren, or ill health, we would tell each other, and ourselves, that we were glad that we had *stuck it out*.

In recent years, whenever we touched each other, I had a fleeting intimation that we had both been frozen, thawed out, and repackaged as husband&wife. But we did touch. Sometimes out of lust. Sometimes for an easy life. And sometimes because it was pleasant to do so.

Humans derive more comfort than we should from routine, habit, the small satisfactions of the everyday, and we know it, and we are secretly ashamed.

I am tired.

I let each vertebra nestle deeper into the foam of the car seat. I have no sense now of how I look or act, only a feeling that I am my own distilled essence, with no clear form in space, comfortable being quiet, unresponsive.

Huw is also silent.

Too much has already been said between strangers who feel they have known each other for a long time. And I already know that we will never speak like this again, that it was not the beginning of something, just a rare connection in time, too precious to forget, too flimsy to build anything on.

His voice when he speaks again startles me.

—It will get bumpier from here.

The car slows and I become alert once more, the way you do when you know that you are reaching the end of something. Then we turn off the narrow road that we have been on for some time, and into a laneway.

—Here we are.

When the car stops, I see the outline of a pebbledash cottage through the windscreen. There is no red door or thatched roof or geraniums in pots. But I no longer care about appearance. At least, not in the ways that I once might have. I sense immediately a kinship with the cottage. It is neglected, a little lonely. But it's fine for a week or two.

I am reluctant to get out of the car, as though opening the door will break some spell. But Huw is already out, and it is too dark to see anything once the headlights are switched off.

I hear the clank of the boot opening and Huw saying something to the dog in Welsh.

At the cottage door, Huw hands me three keys on a steel ring, and stands back.

—The Yale is for the front door. The others are for inside.

The Yale is stiff in the lock, but after a few turns the door opens onto a porch that has been painted many times, a thick cream gloss.

The brass knob on the interior door twists easily. Inside, a cast iron fireplace. A carpeted floor. White-washed walls. A sofa. A small table with two chairs. Shelves built into an alcove. An open staircase. The carpet is worn, and the ceiling has a sag in it. The walls are weather-stained in places. Along the mantelpiece there is a line-up of what my mother would have called gewgaws, all covered in dust: porcelain figurines, a red clock with no battery, a pottery vase with nothing in it, two old black flat irons, a snow globe with GREETINGS

FROM TENBY written on the base. And at either end, candle holders containing candle stubs.

The cold hits me and I try not to shiver.

In the galley kitchen, an uncovered LED bulb flickers on, revealing a free-standing electric cooker and an ancient fridge. Another door leads to a bathroom with a pink bath, toilet and sink, a linoleum floor, curled at the edges. Still in its wrapping, a new shower curtain has been placed in the bathtub. Also, a new bath mat folded on the toilet seat.

Huw stands back, leaving me to climb the open staircase alone.

Here, a mezzanine room with a bed, a wardrobe and a chair. Bedlinen stacked on the chair, still in its packaging.

Huw's wife has bought the new items, I guess, but she has not been here herself. She gave him the items and told him to clean everywhere, thoroughly, before he advertised the cottage to rent. And he believes that he has.

Through the window I can decipher only faint shadows, a fenced yard with a small shed and beyond it, the blackness of fields.

My body feels like it is turning to glass.

Downstairs again, I keep my trench coat on while Huw lights the fire. He takes old newspapers from a shelf and tears out pages, rolling them into tight tubes and then knotting each into a circle, before throwing it on the hearth. He does this six times. I hear him talking to the dog as he works, but his voice is far away. He places his paper circles neatly into the grate, three at the front and three behind, laying firelighters in the gaps between them. This structure he covers neatly with kindling, across and behind, like a low building.

—I had that chimney cleaned a few weeks back.
He is talking to me, not the dog.
—A crow's nest had to be taken from one of the pots.

He takes a candle stub from one of the holders on the mantelpiece, places it on the hearth and breaks it into pieces with a penknife, dotting the fragments on the kindling. He lays the coals from a bucket on top of everything, arranging it like a dome. When at last, he puts a match to it all, a fire bursts forth and licks high up into the chimney.

—They made a fuss. I was back a few days later, checking the water tank, and the devils were still circling . . .
His arms make broad arcs in the air.
—That smoke, there. That will clear after a good fire.
He is talking about the crows . . .

Huw takes the blackened wad of toilet paper from his pocket and wipes his hands. There is no more than a foot between the top of his head and the ceiling.

—There's enough coal in the bunker to last the week, but I should order in a day or two. I'll write out the number. Or you can order directly in the village. All smokeless these days, but it lets out a decent heat.

He adds more. About the boiler, about the flush on the toilet, about one of the back rings on the cooker . . .

Then he stops.

—Everything in good time. You'll get the hang of it. The bedroom will need an airing. Probably best to sleep in here to-night. I've done it. Not bad, the sofa. Pull it up nearer the fire.

I want to say that I won't be here long enough for all that, but no words come out of my mouth.

From my pocket, I take the cash that I withdrew from the ATM in the town and hand him £300. I tell him to count the money, to make sure that it is all there. He gives a low laugh that sounds out of practice and says that he trusts me. He adds something else that I don't hear and then hurries out the front door, leaving the dog in the cottage. He returns a minute later, carrying a box from the car. It's the radio that I requested. He must have bought it before he picked me up.

And then he is gone, the dog trotting after him this time.

Outside, the car's engine starts up and its headlights pan slowly down toile curtains, disappear.

It is a relief to be finally alone.

Only the sound of the fire breaks the silence. It is already spreading heat into the room.

I reach under the tasselled shade of a floor lamp and switch it on.

Whatever needs doing – making up the bed or fetching coal – I will do it tomorrow. There is no rush. I have no desire to get anything 'done'.

I pull the sofa nearer to the fire and sit there for a while, getting warm. The floor lamp casts yellow light into shadows.

It is peaceful to look at things without wanting to change them.

Later, I go out to the small galley kitchen. The fridge is a squat, off-white thing with a plastic handle, and it lets out a tiny drone when I open it. I have to hunker down to see inside. The freezer drawer is fuzzed over with frost and there is nothing in there but an old ice tray.

Slowly, I unpack the groceries from the plastic bag.

In the press under the sink, there's a can of motor oil, a few cleaning products, a lunchbox containing batteries and light bulbs, an old steel wool pad and a brass doorknob. The oddly shaped spaces around the U-bend are veiled in cobwebs.

I think about opening the bottle of wine, having a drink.

Maybe later.

I put it in the press with the wash-up liquid.

From the Formica counter, I take a steel kettle, fill it and switch it on. The kettle rattles into service, gains purchase, gets louder and louder until finally, it clicks. I make tea in a mug and twiddle with the dial on the new radio until I find a classical music station, which I leave on at a low volume.

There is no bin in the kitchen. And the water from the hot tap is cold. The glass in the window above the sink has a crack in it. What about waste disposal? And the immersion?

Everything in good time.

The grill on the cooker works and I make toast, put butter and marmalade on, and eat it sitting on the sofa, drinking a mug of tea. The fire is hot now but I still have my trench coat on. I take the phone from my pocket, turn it on. The internet connection symbol is still there, but the signal strength is down to one bar.

I turn it off.

Tomorrow I will dispose of it.

I am tired of WhatsApp messages and text messages and Skype calls and phone calls. I am not going to miss work emails. I am not going to miss 'Recommended For You' from global tech companies that I say I am going to boycott and never do. And I am not going to download the digital voucher at the starred thread of emails between myself and a hotel manager in the West of Ireland, arising out of a complaint I made that the room we stayed in was below standard.

I am not going to be that woman anymore.

The toilet seat in the bathroom is icy and I have to bang the handle a few times before it flushes, and the cistern takes an age to fill. At the sink, the taps are stiff. The water that spills out is slightly discoloured, but I brush my teeth anyway, pat some water on my face, dry it with one of the new turquoise towels.

I unpack the rolled-up duvet from upstairs, spread it over the sofa, and undress down to my T-shirt, knickers and socks. When I lie down, the upholstery moulds beneath me and I can smell mustiness, but I am warm. The sounds of the country drift towards me and I feel at peace.

Somewhere out there, in a few hours, dawn will come up on neat-cut lawns and wildflower meadows, birds will chirr in the branches of pruned trees. And at the edge of things, in the shadows, a young fox will slink away before alarms go off in identical houses.

There is a shuttering of images as I drift towards sleep. Tom, in a suit, rescuing me from a crowded gig. Lauren turning clumsy cartwheels in the garden. Mark clinging to me when I pick him up from crèche.

In darkness, all losses seem possible.

Last week two strangers called to the cottage.

It was a fine day after a string of rainy ones and I was working in the garden, planting tulip bulbs in an old bath that I had found in the shed.

When I heard the dog barking and then a loud knock, I got a fright. No one comes to the door except Huw and Lena, and the dog doesn't bark at them. In fact, he goes completely nuts for Lena, rolling over like a puppy so she can pet his belly.

The callers were women in their thirties with London accents.

I invited them in and made tea. They spoke passionately about farmers poisoning the land, about E. coli in tap water, about ghost fishing, about the castration of male piglets without anaesthetic. They explained that they blocked motorways to prevent cars from spreading their poisonous fumes, defaced artworks to raise awareness. One of them, a young woman with acne, declared that she would rather die than sit back and do nothing while the world went up in flames. They asked if I wanted to attend their next meeting. I said no and they left in silence, leaving mud marks behind on the rug.

I have no energy for fighting. Everything is breaking down, yes, but it has *always* been breaking down, I wanted to tell them. There is not much anyone can do but leave as little trace as possible on the Earth when they die. And tell no more lies, I wanted to add. And love people as much as they can. But I have already failed at that.

I miss Elaine.

I tried phoning her once on the old Nokia that Lena gave me. I found her landline on one of the computers in the library.

—YOU HAVE REACHED THE VOICEMAIL OF . . .
[Father Voice] —*The Barrett family* . . .
[Elaine's Voice] —*cannot come to the phone right now.*
[Child Voice 1] —*So leave a message,*
[Child Voice 2] —*but short and sweet or we'll press delete.*
I hung up.

Sometimes a thought pops into my head and Elaine is the only person in the world I want to share it with. But the woman I am missing is a fictional character – irreverent and funny, an amalgam of Elaine between the ages of nine and thirty-nine – and not the woman who exists now.

People change. We lose bits of ourselves and get new bits, until one day two old friends who meet in a restaurant are nothing but shadow puppets to each other, both trying to resuscitate a connection that died years ago, leaving each other with a strange rage that over time morphs back into ghost-love.

Every so often Elaine sends me a postcard of a famous painting. She must have asked Tom for the address. The same thing is written on each one: *Thinking of you. E.* I have put them on the mantelpiece behind the red clock. At night, when I'm sitting at the fire, I sometimes take them down and look at them. My favourite is *The Flight into Egypt* by Rembrandt.

It is the thought of ordinary things that pain me the most.

Mark arriving home to an empty house.

Lauren in a flat cleaning up after the cat.

Tom wheeling a too-large trolley around the supermarket, remembering harissa paste, but forgetting to buy milk.

But if I went back now to that house in the suburbs, I would be no use to anyone.

I am different now.

And so are they.

Mark had changed when he came to see me in August. He was taller and stronger, but it was more than that. His eyes had a flicker of curiosity in them that I hadn't seen for years.

I have had no communication from Lauren, however.

It somehow seems worse for a mother to fail a daughter.

When I asked Mark how she was, he looked at me as if to say *ask her yourself*, which was fair. He did mention that he had the attic bedroom now and that his dad and someone called Vikki had helped soundproof the walls so that he could play drums in there. It was his friend, when I was showing her the hen coop later, who explained that Lauren had taken her cat and moved in with her girlfriend. I recognised the girlfriend's name – Anna – as that of the girl with the baby-blue Fiat 500. Apparently they'd been together on and off for years.

Tom and I speak on the phone regularly now. It is good to hear his voice, but the next time we meet in person will be to sign divorce papers. Sometimes, on the phone, there's a pause and I know that part of him is still waiting for an explanation.

But I have no explanation for what happened. Just remnants of memory to be sifted through. A pair of my husband's shoes tucked under the table in the hallway, their thin laces hanging from them like tails, the steamy sweet smell of the bathroom after my daughter had taken a shower, the way my son liked nothing more than to play football with the other boys on summer evenings. A memory. The green area of the estate on that last morning when I drove past it, a discarded football yellow in the car headlights.

When I wake sometimes in the early hours, I imagine that I am still living in the house in the suburbs. In my mind, I run over the rooms, the garden, the estate, remembering what they were like and how they looked at different times of the year. And other times, when I can't sleep, I take off the front of the house like a doll's house, and peer in, trying to see what it is like now. Does Anya still come every Tuesday? Did Tom go ahead with our plans to renovate the main bathroom? Is there still a bottle of wine in the corner cabinet?

That day when I thought I saw Tom in the village, I wanted so much for it to be him, for time to collapse and him to be standing awkwardly at a gig, dressed in a suit, and me saying *rescue me* all over again. When it was good with Tom, it was better than anything. It is easy to want to forget that.

I lost all my photos when I disposed of my phone. But I don't miss them, even the ones of the children when they were younger. Photos don't aid memory, they overpower it. They recall what no longer exists. Memory allows us to gently forget the sadness of losing everything to time.

On good days part of me imagines that I can repair my mistakes from all those years in the past, when I froze in the face of my daughter's pain, my son's pain. But there is no going back, only forward.

Recently the faces of the two children on the train to Rosslare, the ones with the shouty father, have morphed into Lauren and Mark – his sensitive eyes, the world already too much for them, her steely fragility. I would like to sit with one of them either side of me, read to them, colour in pictures with them, treat them to hot chocolates when the girl comes around with the trolley.

I would like to stay on the train with them forever.

There are days when loss is everywhere, attached to no particular thing – to my clothes hanging on the line, to a small collection of second-hand books on the shelf in the alcove, to the wildflowers in a vase on the table. But nothing lasts. Soon the sense of loss fades, and the world returns to nothing much at all. It is easier than it should be not to think about people you love.

Whatever needs doing in the cottage – replacing, painting, mending – I do it slowly, making as little alteration as possible, and I go gently, as you might wash an old person, attentively, bit by bit. There is no rush. I have no desire to get anything 'done'.

Last summer, when I was working in the garden, I found a caterpillar eating the leaves of the geraniums I had planted. I was about to throw it in the compost when I thought, *What the hell am I doing? Killing a butterfly so that I can have flowers in a pot?*

Yesterday, Lena arrived at the cottage. I had invited her to drop by, but I didn't think that she would. She came round the back to where I was hunched over shovelling coal from the bunker and hollered at me before I saw her.

—I am fucking dying for a coffee.

I nearly fell over with fright.

In the kitchen I offered her tea, but she produced a bottle of wine from her rucksack and we drank it in the living room chatting by the fire. Then we made cheese toasties with the rattling grill and I remembered the bottle of wine in the press under the sink, a bit dusty after a year, but fine. We drank it as the night fell outside. The dog had wormed his way onto the sofa beside Lena and shuddered from time to time as she stroked its ear. I looked forward to sleeping next to the warmth of Lena's body, to kissing her, to holding her close, but I knew that we would not have sex. All that energy between us . . . why convert it?

It is morning now, and Lena has gone.

I walk to the village to buy some bread and milk.

It is very still and the trees look astonishing.

How have I never seen trees in this way before?

I feel it now as I once did, not a desire to make art, but the delight that comes when the senses are fully open to beauty and wonder, to the aliveness of the world. And what I want now is to remain in this state, as much as is possible, not be expelled back into the world of hours.

It occurs to me, walking along a country road in Wales in November, with the sky blue and the trees black and the dog rummaging in a hedge somewhere up ahead of me, that this probably *is* just one more 'story' about a woman who was 'imbalanced' or who had everything and wanted MORE.

But even if that's true, I am not going to swallow arsenic or jump in front of a train.

And the door shuts at the beginning, not the end.

Acknowledgements

Thanks go to:

Lettice Franklin and all at W&N;

Matthew Turner at RCW;

The Arts Council of Ireland;

Danny Denton, Eibhear Walshe and all at UCC Creative Writing;

Declan Meade, Thomas Morris, Phyl Herbert, Selina Guinness, Nathan O'Donnell, Aoife Tunney, Dimitra Xidous;

Lucy, Oisín and Georgiana.